CLOCKWORK CRAZY

by
Elle Strauss

Elle Strauss

CLOCKWORK CRAZY
by Elle Strauss
Copyright © 2015 Elle Strauss
Cover by Steven Novak

ESB Publishing

The stress created by Casey's recent split from Nate causes her to trip back in time in a haphazard manner, and not always to the same time! Sometimes she's in 1929 Boston getting more entangled than ever with the mishaps of her new and not-so-helpful friends, and at other times she's back in 1775 trying to make sure the colonists still win the war of Independence!

Will the craziness ever stop? And will she and Nate work out things in time for graduation?

Chapter One

It is better to have loved and lost than never to have loved at all.

What a bunch of crock!

And the old adage was certainly no comfort to me as I curled up in the middle of some random farmer's field, bawling my eyes out. I snotted up my sleeve wanting to curse every silly love song and romantic soliloquy I'd ever heard. The people who wrote those words were *liars*. Heartbreak was explosive, wrenching, and annihilating. It battered and whipped and taunted the one afflicted by it. It crushed me like an avalanche of ragged stones without the decency to actually kill me. The pain was so deep and thorough I felt like someone was peeling off my skin.

I hated, hated, *hated* that I had known love. It was so much better for me when love was a fairy tale. I wished with all my bruised and bleeding heart that I'd never stopped *hating* Nate back in my sophomore year.

This present agony was all his fault! If he hadn't accepted a dare to dance with me at that stupid Fall Dance (I took back the forgiveness I'd extended to Lucinda for tricking me into going), and hadn't tripped with me back to the nineteenth century, and hadn't let my infatuation turn into love—and worse, if he hadn't loved me back—I'd be happily unaware of this torment and probably half-heartedly dating Austin King. I'd be graduating in a few weeks with my body, soul, and spirit in one piece and in complete and wonderful ignorance.

Ignorance was *totally* underrated.

What you don't know won't hurt you—how true! I wanted to start a campaign to warn other high school girls: study, get good grades and for God's sake, leave the boys alone!

I let out another low moan. I could have blamed Nate, but really, the mess I was in was totally all my fault. I had known it would be hard to have a boyfriend in college while I was still in high school. I had known there would be "college girls," vipers who were more aggressive and experienced with boys than me. I had thought I was up to the challenge, but Fiona "the Floozy" Friaz, Latin beauty and head cheerleader to Nate's basketball team, had proven to be my match. She hadn't even tried to pretend that she wasn't after my boyfriend. Even though Nate reassured me over and over again that she was not a threat, I let her get under my skin.

In my defense, she had made it personal, tweeting her intentions straight to me!

When Nate announced that his basketball team was going to Spain for a tournament, and that Floozy would be going, my insecurities hit high gear. To make things worse, I couldn't tag along. With my condition, I can't fly long distances, especially overseas.

Nate had promised me all my firsts, but international travel was something he could never give me. No one could.

It had killed me that Fiona would have this experience with Nate instead of me. And I had no doubt she would be *with* Nate.

So what did I do? I signed up for a class trip to Hollywood. Even though we were flying from Boston to LA, I had been certain—fairly—that I would be fine so long as I slept. I never tripped (my word for time travel) while sleeping. It wasn't that long of a flight (unlike going to Spain), and it would give me something to focus on other than *Nate and Fiona.*

What I hadn't counted on was Austin King. For some unfathomable reason, Austin, a good-looking guy in my creative writing class and part of the group going to Hollywood, decided that he was interested in me. Austin was the kind of guy who went after what he wanted, and any hurdle in the way was just a challenge that heightened his competitiveness. (Just like Fiona!)

By the time I got to Hollywood, Nate's lack of attentiveness and Austin's abundance of attention left me feeling angry and confused. When Floozy posted a picture of her with her arms draped over my boyfriend, I died inside.

Austin pulled me into a hug to comfort me, and that led to my biggest mistake of all. I let him kiss me— *and I kissed him back.*

I was messed up! I ran away from Austin and straight into Adeline Savoy, another time traveler from Hollywood, and we both tripped together. Only, we didn't go to either one of our usual time travel loops (which was 1863 for me, 1957 for her), but reset to a brand new loop: 1929.

We'd gone back to the present and I returned to Cambridge, but then I had tripped again, by myself.

Which was how I got to where I was now.

"Casey?"

I'd been so tangled up in my ball of woe, I hadn't heard anyone approach. I quickly wiped my face with the bottom of my shirt, dabbed at my eyes and drew my fingers through my runaway curls. I turned to the girl's voice and gawked at Lolly Kavanaugh.

Lolly had picked me up when I was hitch-hiking on a previous trip to 1929 and had become a friend of sorts. I'd only ever seen her dressed fashionably in flashy, flapper-style dresses. At this moment she wore oversized field trousers held up with suspenders and a blue button-down blouse. Two scruffy mid-sized dogs sniffed the ground around her. A tractor was parked in the distance.

"Casey, is that you?" she asked. "Are you all right?"

I jumped to my feet and brushed the dirt off my jeans, keeping my bloodshot eyes averted. "Yeah. I'm okay." A hiccup betrayed me.

She shook her messy brunette bob and popped a hand on her hip. "Those are the strangest work clothes I've ever seen."

I wore a striped red and navy blue T-shirt, skinny jeans, and canvas running shoes. My backpack lay at my feet. Unfortunately, it only contained my homework, not any costumes for this period.

"Uh, yeah. These are... my brother's. They don't really fit." The excuse sounded lame, even to me, but I couldn't come up with anything better in my current, weakened emotional state.

I stared at my empty hands and gasped. Nate's pocket watch was missing. I must've dropped it. I fell back to my knees and examined the ground around me, turning over stones and pushing aside carrot tops. The earth clung to my nails as I groped. Nothing.

I leaned back on my heels and let out a long sigh as I absorbed yet another blow. I must've dropped it on Nate's front step.

"What are you looking for?" Lolly asked.

"I thought I'd dropped something, but..." I brushed soil off my knees as I stood up. "Is this your farm?" I asked. I was used to coincidence and chance in my way of life, so the fact that Lolly stood in front of me just now almost didn't surprise me.

"Yeah. How'd you find it? Were you looking for me?"

I sniffled and turned away to take in the open pastures and farmland that would one day be the neighborhood Nate Mackenzie lived in.

"I'm kind of lost."

"Forgive me, but you do look it. Why don't you come back to the house with me and you can tell me what's wrong. And please don't insult my intelligence by saying that there's nothing wrong. You look a mess, darlin'."

Lolly whistled for the dogs and started toward the tractor. I picked up my modern backpack and followed.

"It's a one-seater," she said, hopping onto the wide seat, "but it's big enough for you to slip in behind me."

I placed my foot on a runner and heaved myself up behind Lolly. The tractor stuttered and popped as Lolly turned the engine over, stepped on the clutch and put it into gear. We puttered toward a farmhouse in the distance and I was glad the motor was too loud to talk over. I had approximately five minutes to get my story straight before Lolly began her interrogation in earnest. Though I'd only known her for a short time, I knew she would be relentless in her quest for answers.

We approached a small farmhouse painted canary yellow. Large trees in a sea of leafy green surrounded it like a big protective hug. Several out-buildings—sheds, barns... and outhouse?—sat just beyond. Lolly pulled the tractor into a shady spot behind one of them and killed the engine.

"We'll have to sneak you upstairs and get you out of those rags," she said. "Ma's very conservative and won't appreciate that you're wearing dungarees that are much, much too small for you. Though," she added with a sympathetic glance at my clothing choice, "you can't be to blame if you've outgrown your work clothes and your family can't afford to buy you new ones that fit properly. Did you say you were the eldest?"

I didn't remember what I'd told her about my family. I'd learned it was best to stick with the truth whenever possible.

"Yes."

"Obviously you've been crying. Once we're settled, you're going to tell me all about it."

A line of laundry hung in the back yard with large white sheets floating in the breeze like sails. Lolly ducked low as we followed along and motioned for me to do the same. "In case Ma's looking out the window," she explained.

Lolly carefully opened a screen door, nodded with her head that I should enter first, and then she slowly let the door close without a sound. I had the feeling Lolly was skilled and experienced at sneaking in and out of her house.

We paused at the base of a narrow flight of stairs.

"Follow my steps exactly," Lolly whispered. She strategically placed her foot on one side of a step and then the other—sometimes in the middle, a pattern that got us to the second floor without a squeak.

We stepped inside a small bedroom with ceilings that sloped sharply to the windows. There was only a narrow section where I could stand up straight and not bump my head. Lolly chuckled. "It's helps that I'm short. At least when it comes to getting dressed in this room.

Despite its diminutive size, the room was cozy, with floral wallpaper that ran from the wood floor to the cream-colored ceiling. White sheers floated lazily around the open windows. Lolly opened a darkly stained wooden wardrobe that rested against the longest portion of an interior wall and removed a couple of dresses. She held a flowing rosy-pink one out to me.

"I hope it fits," she said. "It drops to my ankles on me, so it should easily fall to your shins."

She unabashedly stripped out of her farm trousers revealing a conservative set of undergarments that would blush at the sight of my comparatively skimpy underthings. There wasn't much I could do about that and Lolly was busy in front of her vanity mirror, fixing her hair, so I didn't think she'd notice. I slipped out of my jeans and T-shirt, pushed them under Lolly's bed with my toe and wiggled into her dress. We were both of slender build and the loose style made way for any differences in body shape. And, as Lolly predicted, the dress landed at my shins.

"Can I borrow a brush and a few pins?" I asked. I ducked to get a glimpse of myself in the mirror and stared at my blotchy face and red-rimmed eyes. No matter how badly I felt right now I had to stop crying, at least until I was home again and in the privacy of my own room.

Lolly pointed to all her hair accessories. "Sure thing."

I remembered how Adeline had made a faux bob out of my long hair the first time we'd tripped back to 1929 in Hollywood. My version wasn't nearly as neat, but it would do. My real problem wasn't my hair, but my feet. There was no way my hoofs would fit into any of Lolly's petite shoes.

I pointed a toe. "I'm going to have to go barefoot." Unless I wore my sneakers.

Lolly's eyes widened in shock at my pronouncement. I gathered a lady without stockings or footwear was a little too much for this "modern" girl.

"My mother has large feet, too. I take after my father's side of the family," she added quickly. Before saying more she disappeared out of the room. I took the opportunity to dig into her cosmetics, knowing from my previous encounter that Lolly wouldn't mind. In fact, I knew she'd insist, and for the first time I wondered where we were getting ready to go out to. I packed it on to even out my skin tone and hoped that plenty of eye makeup would detract from the puffiness.

Lolly returned with a really unattractive pair of brown tie-up shoes—very sensible. She smiled apologetically. "Sorry, this is the best I can do."

"It's fine," I said. It wasn't like I was trying to impress anyone, anyway. "I assume we're going somewhere?"

"Marlene's throwing a party. I promised her I'd come. Won't she be surprised to see you again!"

"Won't she!" I said it with a touch of sarcasm. Marlene Charter was the first person I'd met in 1929

Boston. Nate was with me on that trip (and very angry with me that I'd caused a reset). We ended up at a speakeasy in hopes of finding a way to make money when Marlene offered me a job dancing.

It would've been fine, except I had been spotted by Sheldon Vance, a mob thug who'd duped me and Adeline on our reset loop to 1929 Hollywood into helping him film a movie, which turned out to be a front for an actual bank robbery! Marlene had taken us in after Nate was injured in the subsequent scuffle. I didn't like how she blatantly flirted with Nate, and she hadn't liked how we left without saying good-bye or thank-you after accepting her hospitality. Time travel doesn't always allow for social niceties.

Since then Marlene had begrudgingly helped me by getting me a job in the speakeasy kitchen. However, she was probably less than impressed that I had taken off (again) before finishing my last shift. Not only had the poor young helper, Paul Junior, been left alone to do all the clean up, he was probably freaked out at seeing me disappear into thin air like that.

Lolly handed me a strand of long beads, and I slipped them over my head. She looked at me like I was a project she wasn't quite finished with but didn't know what else to do with. "Let's go."

I followed her exact pattern down the steps to the back door. She opened it and motioned me to go outside. "I'll be right there," she whispered. "Stay out of sight."

"Ma!" she called. "I'm going into town."

13

"Lolita! You hold on now!" Her mother's voice filtered outside. "You're not going into town dressed like that!"

"Ma, we've been through this a hundred times. This is how kids dress nowadays."

"It just makes you look so... cheap. Did you forget that Thomas Burgess is coming for dinner tonight? I need your help to prepare things."

"Thomas? Again? Ma...."

"Lolita, don't you lip me!"

"But, Pa promised I could have the car to go into town today."

"Fine, go if you must, but be home by five o'clock, do you hear? I mean it young lady."

The door slammed and Lolly scurried past me in a huff. I hurried after her. "Is everything all right?"

"No! We're not going to be able to stay for Marlene's party. She's going be so angry!"

We came to a narrow garage and I recognized the jalopy inside from the first time Lolly had picked me up. I climbed into the passenger seat. "Your dad lets you take the car out a lot."

"Yeah. He's scared to drive in the city. Figures someone should drive it. Ma's still mad at him for buying it in the first place, but I simply adore him for it."

Once Lolly had backed us out safely, I asked, "Who's Thomas?"

"He's the farmer's son next door. Our parents want to join our farms because they think it's the only way to make the most of the booming economy. The truth is, we bought a flashy new tractor and other machinery with easy money from the bank. They're more expensive to run and though we can do everything faster, we still can't produce enough to make the loan payments."

"What do you mean by join the farms? They want you to marry him?"

"Yes. I'm an only child and a girl. My parents wanted a lot of kids, but…well, they only got me, unfortunately. We have to hire help, but cash flow isn't there for that. Thomas is the eldest of ten kids, and eligible to marry. He could run our farm." She let out a long, sad sigh. "He's a nice enough fellow, but I don't love him." She pressed her shoulders back and said boldly, "I'm not going to marry him. I'm a modern girl!"

Lolly geared down as she came to the intersection at the main road into Boston. "Now, enough about me," she said with an arched brow. "I want to know why you were crying your eyes out in the middle of my field. And don't skip a thing!"

Chapter Two

Nate broke up with you?"

I'd already gone through this agonizing scenario with Lolly, and now Marlene demanded a repeat performance. Only, where Lolly was full of compassion and empathy, Marlene stood with hands on hips and eyes narrowed in scrutiny.

"Well, if you take off without warning with him to do God knows what like you do with your job, then no wonder. I don't doubt that you deserved it."

I was glad I hadn't told them about the kiss with Austin. I'd be tied to a stake and burned.

"Marlene!" Lolly's mouth dropped open in disbelief. "Have a heart!"

Marlene softened slightly at her reproach and her arms dropped to her side. "Well, she did just run off and leave the restaurant in a lurch."

That was what she called Vance's speakeasy? A restaurant?

Lolly huffed. "I'm sure she had her reasons."

I was warmed by Lolly coming to my defense.

"It's okay," I said. I sat on Marlene's bed and rested my head against the wall. "She's not totally wrong. Nate had every reason to break things off. I'm actually surprised it hasn't happened before now."

I wiped at a tear escapee. "It just hurts so much."

Lolly settled in beside me and gave me a perky look. "There, there. Let it out and then let it go. Who needs a fella anyway? We're modern girls!"

Marlene surprised me by lighting up a cigarette.

Lolly's eyes widened. "When did you become a smoke eater?"

Marlene held up a half-empty carton of smokes. "Sheldon left his pack on the table at work."

Lolly reached for it. "Butt me." Lolly lit up and let out a puff a smoke before giving into a coughing fit. I was tempted to open up another window.

Marlene ignored her unladylike display and eyed me as I sat curled up pitifully on her bed. "Lolly's right," she said after a long smoky exhale. "No sense crying over spilled milk. Nate was a good chap, but there are plenty others."

I know they were trying to comfort me, but it wasn't working. Not by a mile. The ache in my chest

17

throbbed like a living entity, growing and pressing against my ribs. I wrapped my arms tightly around my chest hoping I could keep it together. These girls weren't my BFFs. I didn't want to pour my heart out to them. I wanted Lucinda.

Lolly changed the subject. "How are the party plans, Mar?"

Marlene tapped ash into a decorative ashtray. "Nifty. Sheldon is helping me. His caterers and decorators should be arriving any moment."

"Your mother is okay with this?" I asked. I'd only met Mrs. Charters once, but she was anything but progressive and I couldn't imagine her condoning a party in her house. Or smoking in the bedroom.

"Of course not," Marlene said sharply, like I was a dimwitted child. "She's in New York visiting my sister." Marlene crossed her arms, raising the hand with the cigarette. The plume billowed over her blond head. "I have the whole place to myself."

"Is Sheldon coming?" Lolly said. She'd put out her half-smoked cigarette and climbed onto the bed. I got the impression her smoking session had left her light-headed. She wrapped her arms around a big pillow and rested on her side with her head propped up on one hand. "He's a little old for your friends, isn't he?"

"He's not even thirty, Lolly. You act like that's ancient. And yes, he's coming later." She wiggled her brows. "If you know what I mean."

"Marlene!" Lolly exclaimed again. "You have to be careful. He's an *experienced* man."

18

Marlene pressed her cigarette butt into the ashtray until the ember went out, then shot Lolly a look. "Oh, don't be such a killjoy. Besides, you're the one who's always going on about how we're modern women." She checked her perfect finger waves in the mirror before leaving Lolly and me alone. "I think I heard the doorbell."

Lolly sat up when she left. "I'm so worried about her. That Sheldon Vance fella makes me uneasy. I think he's involved in something illegal."

"I think you're right." I knew she was right.

"We need to find a way to expose him, Casey. If Marlene knew what he was up to, she'd toss him like dirt on her shoe."

I wasn't so sure about that. My guess was Marlene was more like Sheldon than Lolly would like to believe.

"I wish Ma hadn't planned this dumb dinner with Thomas. Then I'd stay the night and make sure there were no shenanigans between Marlene and Sheldon."

"I could stay," I said.

Lolly clapped her hands. "That would be perfect. But, won't your family worry?"

"I'll call them, it'll be fine."

"You have a phone on the farm?"

Oops. "Uh, yeah, just got one."

"I didn't think phone lines ran out of town."

"Our farm is right on the border." Oh, brother. "Will Marlene let me stay?" I asked, wanting to bring Lolly back to topic.

"I'll convince her to let you stay. Just because I have to go, doesn't mean you should miss out on the fun."

She tilted her head and smiled sympathetically. "And who needs cheering up more than you!"

We heard voices downstairs and Lolly motioned me to follow her. "I can't stay for the party, but I can at least take in the set up."

The kitchen and living room were buzzing with people bringing in supplies and setting up the party atmosphere. The women were dressed much like Lolly and I were, with loose, colorful day dresses that ended below the knees. The guys wore white button-down shirts tucked into high-waist trousers.

Decorations were hung and food displayed, but all I could see in my mind's eye was Nate lounging on the sofa. Or sitting for breakfast at the table. He'd been here with me when I was here last and the memories were like searing blades.

"Are you okay?" Lolly asked. "You look like you've seen a ghost."

I shook my head, hoping to rattle some sense into it. "I'm fine."

Marlene moved about, giving orders in a confident manner. She hadn't yet lost her fortune, an event that she wouldn't experience for another four months. I hoped she'd keep her stamina and strong will once that happened.

She stood beside Lolly and me as she studied her handiwork. "Whatcha think?"

"Looks great," I said. "How many people do you think will come?"

"I dunno. Maybe fifty."

Lolly spun to face her. "Fifty people! Your mother is going to kill you."

"My mother will never know. It's copacetic, Lolly. You worry too much."

"Well, make that one hundred and one," Lolly said. "Casey is staying over. That's all right, isn't it?"

"No, it's not! Lolly, you can't just invite your friends to stay over at other people's houses!"

Ouch. I guess that confirmed that Marlene no longer considered me a friend.

Lolly linked her elbow with Marlene's and spoke gently. "I just don't want you to be alone. It's not safe. If I could stay I would..."

"How's it not safe? And how could she protect *me*? She's the one who seems to get into trouble all the time."

Marlene had a point there.

"I'm worried about Sheldon. He's a man who's interested in you. You shouldn't be alone overnight."

Marlene threw her palms into the air. "That's exactly what I'm *not* afraid of, darlin'. No, you must take your charity case home with you. She's not welcome here one second once you leave."

Double ouch!!

Marlene cut me a haughty glare, knowing she'd spoken loud enough for me to hear. I almost saluted her. Message received. Over and out.

Suddenly I heard Sheldon's baritone voice. "I hear there's a party going on?"

Marlene hurried to the entrance to greet him, and he kissed her on both cheeks. "Baby, you look amazing," he said.

She purred back. "So do you."

Lolly leaned into me. "I thought he wasn't coming until later."

"I don't think he trusts her to be alone," I said. "I've seen them together before." I didn't say from where. I wasn't quite ready to betray Marlene's confidence about the speakeasy. "He's pretty clingy."

"Is he really going to hang out with a bunch of kids?"

I shrugged. "My guess is that he's going to supply drinks."

Lolly pointed to the dining room table. "There's already punch and soda."

"Not those kind of drinks."

Lolly gasped. "You mean alcohol?"

I nodded. "And make a pretty penny doing it as well."

Sheldon Vance scoured the room and I spun on my heels, turning my back to him before he saw my face.

Lolly's brow buckled. "What's eating you?"

"I don't want him to see me here."

"You *know* him? You've met Sheldon Vance? Why have I not heard this before? I haven't even been officially introduced."

"Believe me, you're not missing out on anything." I stared down at her. "Is there another way out? If we're not staying, now would be as good a time as any to go."

"Yeah, through the kitchen. I'll meet you there. Marlene would kill me if I left without saying goodbye."

Chapter Three

Lolly fussed so much over Marlene the whole ride home, I was getting sick of hearing her name.

"Marlene and I have been good friends since grade school."

"Marlene was always so sensible and responsible."

"Marlene took the passing of her pa really hard. They were quite close. Marlene doesn't have that with her mother."

"Marlene has changed since meeting Sheldon Vance. She's so full of secrets now."

"I hate how Marlene makes me feel like I'm still a child. She's gotten so full of herself lately."

Her driving was jerky in her agitated state, and I held onto the door handle with white knuckles—especially as we traveled over the bridge that crossed the Charles River into Cambridge.

We finally arrived at Lolly's farm and this time she had to introduce me to her family—unless she planned to hide me away in her room again. There was no point to that, and I was grateful.

"I brought a friend home," Lolly called as we entered through the back door near the kitchen. Mrs. Kavanaugh approached with a towel in hand. She was taller than her daughter, with broad shoulders for a woman, and thick around the stomach. Her expression was tight with anxiety and I squirmed a little under her scrutiny.

"This is Casey," Lolly said. "I met her at Marlene's."

Mrs. Kavanaugh forced a smile. "Welcome." I had the feeling she didn't like the fact that Lolly had brought a female friend to dinner, someone who might cause Thomas to fail to be single-minded about her daughter.

"The two of you can help with meal preparation." Mrs. Kavanaugh opened a drawer and pulled out two aprons. "Put these on." She eyed me carefully. "I trust you know your way around a kitchen."

This kitchen was quarter the size of the Donovan family kitchen, and the appliances were antiquated. Not even new for this decade. I just nodded and then followed Lolly around like a puppy, taking my cues from her. I didn't understand how to work the stove, but washing dishes in the sink was a universal chore. I set to work scrubbing pots.

Mrs. Kavanaugh hadn't held back. She had roasted a chicken *and* a ham, along with garden potatoes, cooked carrots, green beans and pickled beets. A big pot of gravy simmered on the back burner.

She'd been busy baking, too. Three apple pies sat on one of the narrow countertops. My stomach growled loudly and I realized it'd been a whole day since I'd last had a proper meal.

The farmhouse was small but tidy. A buffet sat along the back wall of the dining area and Lolly pointed to the plates and cutlery. "Do you mind setting the table?"

"For how many?" I asked. No one had mentioned if anyone was coming with Thomas Burgess.

"Five," she said, as she collected glasses.

Five. An odd number. I hoped I wouldn't stick out too much. That I wouldn't upset the balance.

Mrs. Kavanaugh wrung her hands as she watched the grandfather clock sitting in the corner of the living room. "Where is your father?" she said tightly. "Thomas is going to be here in twenty minutes." She turned to Lolly. "Get upstairs and freshen up! He's looking for a bride not a housemaid."

OMG.

Lolly spun sharply so her mother couldn't see the scowl on her face. "Why shouldn't he see me as a housemaid?" She muttered as she stormed up the steps. "Isn't that really what he's after?"

Lolly removed the dress she was wearing and then stood statue still in her underwear. She might be a modern woman, but her underthings certainly were not. The

26

waistline of her panties practically touched her ribs and the band around her bra was at least an inch wide.

"Lolly?" I asked carefully.

She snapped back to attention. "I'm fine." She approached a washbowl that was set up under the window in her bedroom and wiped her face and neck with a damp cloth. "This charade is just so ridiculous. I don't know why they insist on such a senseless display." She removed another dress from her wardrobe—blue this time—and slipped it over her head. "I don't have to marry for convenience, do I?"

"Of course not!" I said. "You should marry who you want. Marriage is a big commitment and the least you can do to make it happy is to start off by being in love."

Her eyes landed on me for a moment, her face frozen in place like my little speech wasn't possibly a truth for her. "I hope you're right," she finally said.

She then crossed to her wardrobe and produced another dress. "I'm sorry, I don't have another dress for you."

"I'm not the one on display," I said lightly, but Lolly didn't crack a smile.

I did take the opportunity to wash my face and redo my makeup a little. I noticed that Lolly applied hers much more lightly than she had in the past.

Mrs. Kavanaugh called up the stairs. "Lolita!" Her voice was light and pleasant, unlike anything I'd heard from her so far. Lolly noticed, too.

"Thomas is here." She straightened her shoulders. "Let the show begin."

Mr. Kavanaugh was a thin, wiry man who looked like he carried the weight of the world on his bony shoulders. He sat at the head of the table and removed his hat, revealing a greasy, receding hairline. Thomas sat adjacent to him. He was dressed in clean if not fancy clothes—nothing compared to what Sheldon Vance traipsed around in, no matter the time of day. His hair was slicked back and his youthfulness was magnified by the rosiness of his cheeks and the lack of hair on his face. He was a teenager! No wonder Lolly didn't want to marry him.

He stood when he saw Lolly and smiled a good-ol'-boy smile, then blinked when he spotted me appearing from behind. His confusion made it clear that Mrs. Kavanaugh hadn't bothered to mention me.

"Hello, Lolly," he said.

"Hello, Thomas," Lolly returned. "This is my friend, Casey."

"Howdy," he said politely.

"Hi," I returned.

"Lolita," Mrs. Kavanaugh said. "You may have the seat beside Mr. Burgess." Mrs. Kavanaugh sat across from Thomas, and waved to me to take the seat beside her. The atmosphere in the room was thick with awkwardness. Lolly looked put out and sat stiffly, leaning as far away from Thomas as she could without being impolite. Cool waves from Mrs. Kavanaugh washed my way, as if she were afraid my presence would distract Thomas Burgess from the purpose of this dinner. If it weren't for my budding friendship with Lolly, and the fact that I was starving, I would've excused myself and taken off.

We bowed our heads as Mr. Kavanaugh said grace, and the bowls and platters were passed around. I filled my plate.

"So, Casey," Thomas said. "Where are you from? I haven't seen you in these parts before."

Silence descended. Forks paused midair. Mrs. Kavanaugh's brow stretched as if she had been wondering the same thing.

"Just around," I answered feebly.

Mrs. Kavanaugh broke in, returning the direction of the conversation to her daughter. "Lolita prepared the chicken. She's a fine cook, isn't she, Dougal?"

Mr. Kavanaugh cleared his throat. "To my surprise," he said. Mrs. Kavanaugh glared briefly in the direction of her husband. By the look on Lolly's face, I gathered she was surprised, too. From what I could tell in the kitchen, Lolly hadn't cooked anything, though she had done okay at mashing the potatoes.

"Very good," Thomas said, turning slightly to offer Lolly a smile. She didn't return it.

Mrs. Kavanaugh tried again. "Lolly's been busy in the fields. She's gotten really good with that new tractor, hasn't she, Dougal?"

"Ma!" Lolly cried. "Thomas is aware of all my fine qualities. Can we please change the subject?"

Mrs. Kavanaugh's thin lips tightened in disapproval. "Of course." She turned to face me. "Casey, please *do* tell us where you're from, and how you met my daughter?"

Red alert! I had no doubt that Mr. and Mrs. Kavanaugh knew all the farmers in the Cambridge area, and a vague answer wouldn't satisfy them in the way it had Lolly and Marlene.

"What's your last name?" Mr. Kavanaugh asked with sudden interest. "I probably know your pa."

Thomas and Lolly stared at me with wide-eyed interest.

I pressed a cloth napkin to my face and feigned sickness. Actually, I wasn't really faking. I was *dizzy*. "I'm not well," I mumbled as I shifted my chair noisily out from under me. "Excuse me."

I dashed away from the table and out the back door. I could hear Lolly calling after me, but I managed to turn the corner of the house and get out of sight before disappearing into the tunnel of light.

Chapter Four

I trembled as I found myself suddenly standing on Nate's front step, staring at his closed door. The open mouth of the lion on the brass knocker mocked me. It seemed to say, *You've been dumped.*

Once again I was wearing my skinny jeans, striped T-shirt, and spring jacket, my backpack flung over one shoulder.

My hands were empty. Right. Nate's pocket watch. Where was it? I checked the steps and the rose bushes on either side, thinking that maybe I'd tossed it through the air before tripping. Dark soil pushed up under my fingernails. The fleshy part of my palm caught a thorn and I yelped, pressing the wound against my lips. The metallic taste of blood made me wrinkle my face and I blinked back new tears.

31

This was terrible! Why couldn't I find the watch? I was so certain it hadn't come with me to Lolly's field. I'd scoured a good twenty-foot radius there.

I had to leave before Nate came outside again. It would be so humiliating if he found me there, digging around in his mother's flower garden. I lumbered down the street with a throbbing palm and a heart that felt like it was being squeezed in a vice.

Thankfully I didn't have to wait long for the next bus. I dropped coins into the ticket machine and slipped into the first available seat. Then I dug out my phone and texted Lucinda.

Casey: You won't believe what happened to me. Are you free tonight?

I waited for her return text, but when she didn't reply, I put my phone away. She was probably out with Sam Capone. How ironic that just when Lucinda got a boyfriend, I lost mine. No double dating for us!

I leaned my head against the window and pinched my eyelids tight. I just wanted to go home and sleep. Tripping was intensely tiring and I knew I looked like crap with rings around my eyes. That along with the burning sensation of tears threatening to explode didn't make for an attractive look. Best not to subject anyone to that.

The bus lurched to a stop and I hurried down the sidewalk to my house. I kept my head low and my gaze focused on the sidewalk lines. What time was it anyway? Five? Six? I'd just eaten at Lolly's so I wasn't hungry. I hoped mom would be okay with me skipping dinner. She was pretty big on the four of us eating together every night. I'd tell her about Nate and me breaking up. She'd probably be glad to hear it—I knew she thought I was too young to be going out with Nate for so long—but she would sympathize with my broken heart. It was a guaranteed ticket straight to bed. I longed to be horizontal with my nose pressed into my feather pillow.

I heard the sounds of a couple guys bouncing a basketball. We had a hoop in our driveway, but Tim's Corolla blocked my view of the players. An orange ball dropped through the net and a victory hoot followed. My brother didn't play sports anymore since his injury. Did he have friends over to play? That would be a first.

I squinted as I drew closer, and circled around the car. My mouth dropped open. I barely recognized my brother. Not only was his hair buzzed super short, his stance was weighted evenly. He jumped easily to make a two point dunk. Before Tim's injury, he'd been a make-up-wearing, cigarette-smoking Goth. This Tim was a jock!

I clutched at my heart as he performed another lay-up. *Oh no. The timeline had changed again!*

Buzz-cut Tim tucked the ball under his arm and scowled at me. "What are you staring at?"

I tried to blink off my shock. "Nothing, just... who's winning?"

Tim smirked. "I'm cleaning Austin's clock."

Austin? I was so focused on Tim, his athleticism and his new look, I completely missed Austin King! What was he doing here? Why was he playing basketball with my brother?

33

Austin wore a muscle shirt and his well-formed biceps glistened with sweat. He approached me with a friendly smile. "You're late," he said.

Late? For what? "Ah, yeah, I missed the…"

Before I could finish my sentence, Austin's lips were pressed to mine! I froze. How dare he kiss me, and right in front of Tim!

"Hey!" I pushed back on his sweaty chest with my palms.

"What?" he looked genuinely surprised by my reaction. "Tim…" I said.

Tim snorted. "It's not like I haven't seen you guys make out a million times before. You're not exactly discreet."

Yikes. Austin King and I were a *thing?* I swallowed hard. "I gotta go in, um, use the bathroom." I hurried away leaving Austin and Tim to get back to their game.

"What's with her?" I heard Austin ask.

Tim answered, "You never know with my sister. I still don't know what you see in her."

I bristled. Thanks for nothing, Tim!

Mom was in the kitchen, which hadn't changed (at least not noticeably), preparing dinner. She looked the same: short blond hair, petite build, pale skin. I was grateful that some things had remained the same. Dad's overcoats hung in the closet, so bonus! We were still a family.

"Hey, Casey," Mom said, "Can you give me a hand?"

"Actually, Mom, I'm not feeling very well. Is it okay if I lie down for a while?"

She approached me and reached up to touch my forehead. "You look awful. Are you taking your multi-vitamins?"

"I didn't sleep very well last night and today was a busy day at school."

She bobbed her head. "Go get some rest. I'll put a plate away for you."

I reached into my pack for my phone as I climbed the steps to my bedroom. I really hoped that Lucinda and I were friends in this timeline. Maybe that was why she didn't return my text? We weren't friends again? My heart couldn't take another beating. I held my breath as I listened for her voice. She answered on the second ring.

"Lucinda? It's Casey."

"Duh. I saw that on call display. What's up?"

She sounded friendly enough. I thought it best to offer a test. "We're best friends, right?"

"Yeah," she said, stretching the word out like toffee. "Casey, is everything all right?"

The lump in my throat made it hard to breathe. So much had happened since I'd seen her at school. Nate had broken my heart and I'd broken the timeline. Again. "I really need to see you."

"You sound serious. We'll be right over!" Lucinda hung up before I could ask her what she meant by *we*. Maybe we had another friend we hung out with here. I wondered who it could be and if they both knew about my tripping episodes. Maybe this Lucinda didn't know. I was going to have to play it cool. I could at least unload about Nate and how much I wished I hated him right now.

I washed up and changed my clothes—soft things, like yoga pants and an oversized shirt. Once I'd gotten enough comfort from Lucinda, I was going straight to sleep.

The big mystery that needed solving was: what had I done to change the timeline this time? It must've had something to do with Lolly Kavanaugh. Did she marry Thomas because I was there, when without me she wouldn't have? Or vice versa? What influence could she or they possibly have had to make things change?

And, sadly, this time I didn't have Nate to help me figure it out. I lay on my bed and felt my eyes flutter shut. I'd have to leave my investigative work until morning.

A knock on the door roused me back to consciousness and I pulled myself up to a sitting position.

Lucinda's dark head of long, shiny hair poked in through the crack in the door. "Your mom let us in."

Before I had a chance to register who she meant by us, she entered, holding the hand of a tall, green-eyed boy. I felt like throwing up.

It appeared that my Nate Mackenzie was now hers.

Chapter Five

No! I sputtered.

Lucinda's eyes pooled with worry. "Casey, what's wrong?"

You are! You and Nate as a couple are completely wrong!

I cupped my mouth with my hand to keep the horror I felt inside. Lucinda *exchanged a look* with Nate before releasing his hand and taking a spot beside me on the bed.

She asked, "Casey, what happened?"

Nate watched me with little emotion. He didn't know me. Didn't know that he had loved me. All my emotional restrain broke like a dam. I reached for a tissue from the box on my night table and sobbed like mad.

Nate cleared his throat. "Maybe I should wait outside."

37

Lucinda nodded and waved him off.

"You're scaring me, Casey. What happened? Did someone hurt you?"

What a loaded question. Nate hurt me and now Lucinda, by being with Nate. We might be best friends in this time line, but there was no way I could tell her anything now. She might as well be a stranger. In this reality, I had watched a romance bloom between her and Nate, probably cheered her on and helped to make it happen.

I couldn't relate to that Casey, at all.

"How did you and Nate get together?"

Lucinda frowned in confusion. "What do you mean? You were there."

I waved my dirty tissue at her. "I know, just tell me anyway."

"You don't remember? Did you bump your head? You should see a doctor."

I knew I sounded insane, but I had to know. I pleaded again. "Please, just tell me."

"He asked me to dance at the Fall Dance, when you and I were sophomores. You bought the tickets, remember?"

No, I hadn't bought the tickets, she had!

"What about Jessica Fuller?" Jessica had been the head cheerleading mean girl, a sophomore like Lucinda and me, but popular and a boy magnet.

"Jessica? Tim's girlfriend? What about her?"

Oh my trampled heart! Tim was dating Jessica Fuller? Could this day possibly get any worse?

Lucinda smiled softly, but deep lines of concern creased her brow. "I'm going to go get your mom."

"No, wait." I blew my nose like a foghorn. "I'm fine, just, hormonal. Really bad PMS."

Lucinda's brown eyes widened. "This is PMS? On steroids, maybe."

"I know. Crazy, huh. I just need a good night's sleep and I'm sure I'll be fine in the morning."

"You're sure?"

I added a little white lie for good measure. "Yeah. I've had insomnia. It's making me forgetful and emotional." I forced a positive note to my voice. "Nothing a long sleep can't cure."

"Okay." She patted my hand and stood. "Nate and I will pick you up at the usual time for school."

Great. Nate and Lucinda were my ride. I swallowed. "Sure. See you tomorrow."

I didn't move from my spot on my bed, just worked to get my emotional equilibrium back using deep breathing. In for four counts, hold for four, out for four. Repeat. As I focused on my breaths I started to notice my room. Though the bigger things were the same—my furniture, and the way it was set up, my quilt and the curtains on the window—the little things started to come into focus.

Like that the collage of pictures of Nate and me that I had over my desk was missing. My lampshade was purple instead of blue. There was some kind of costume draped over my desk chair. Please, don't tell me I was in the drama club or something.

I curled into a ball, so ready to end this day, when a soft tapping on the door was followed my mother's lithe form.

"Casey?"

"I'm awake," I said.

"Are you ready for a little dinner?"

I could smell the spicy tomato aroma of spaghetti sauce, but my stomach was too knotted to care. "I'm still not feeling well. I'm just going to sleep."

Mom sat on the same spot on the bed Lucinda had recently vacated and the skin around her eyes crinkled slightly as she took me in. "You know you can talk to me, right? About anything."

I knew that. It warmed me that my mother's character hadn't changed from one timeline to the other.

"I know," I said. I would've loved to tell her everything, but I couldn't. This tangle time web was something I'd have to unravel on my own.

I awoke to my alarm the next morning and I stretched lazily enjoying the half-second of ignorance before the truth about the previous day lowered like a boom. I pinched my eyes shut and groaned. Maybe it had all been a bad dream. An unbelievably, realistic nightmare. Maybe this was my real room, and Nate was not with Lucinda but with me. I cracked open the eye closest to my desk hoping to see the Nate-and-Casey collage I'd made last fall. I pouted at the bare spot on the wall.

It wasn't a dream and I was here, in this altered timeline. I was sure that this version of Mom would be on me if I didn't go to school, possibly dragging me to the doctor's. Plus, I didn't want to give Lucinda any reason to keep asking probing questions. I was going to have to go along with things for now.

I dressed, I confess, with a lot of attention to my looks, knowing that I was going to see Nate soon. Even though it meant any effort to gain his attention was a betrayal to Lucinda's friendship, and even though this Nate wasn't my Nate, I couldn't help myself. As far as I was concerned, he should be mine in *every* timeline.

I was surprised to find Dad making breakfast. I knew he could cook, but in my own time he was always at work this time of day.

"Hey," he said when he saw me. "Two poached eggs on toast coming up."

"Thanks, Dad," I said. Dad shoved a plate across the island toward me.

"How come you're not at work?" I asked.

He shot me a look. "Why would I be at work? It's morning."

So, he worked evenings now?

Tim sauntered in at that moment. "Hey weirdo," he said. "Austin wants to know why you blew him off yesterday."

Oh crap! I'd totally forgotten about Austin. "I was sick."

Dad passed Tim his breakfast. Tim grunted in response. I studied my brother more closely as he shovelled his food into the hole on his face.

"Why don't you drive me to school?" I asked.

41

He downed half a glass of orange juice. "What don't you drive yourself?"

I was assuming I didn't have a license or a car since Lucinda and Nate were picking me up. And why wasn't Nate in Boston attending BU?

Tim belched, and shoved off his stool before disappearing through the kitchen door. He didn't even bother to clear his dirty dishes away. Dad took them and loaded them into the dishwasher.

"Where's Mom?" I asked.

His brown fingers tapped along the countertop. "She's at work. Remember, she started her new job yesterday?"

Oh, so Mom didn't work for herself in this world.

I nodded like I had forgotten, and finished the rest of my eggs. "Thanks for the breakfast." I moved around the counter with my dirty dishes, but Dad held out a hand for them before I could load them in the dishwasher.

"I'll do that. You get ready for school."

Ten minutes later I stood at the end of my drive, hair and makeup ready, teeth brushed and school books sorted and in my pack. I had no idea what to expect at school, but I psyched myself up to be ready for anything.

Nate and Lucinda pulled up in Nate's old BMW. Funny how he always drove the same car. My insides folded as I took in the happy couple and opened the door to the backseat. I'd never ridden in the back seat of Nate's car before.

Lucinda was dressed in perky spring colors and had her long hair up in a high ponytail. It swished over her shoulder as she turned to look at me.

"Are you feeling better?" she asked.

My gaze cut to the review mirror. Nate glanced back briefly, his green eyes soft, before backing up onto the street. There was nothing in his eyes that hinted at a hidden desire or longing for me. Clearly, I was the third wheel tag-along in this arrangement.

"Yeah, I'm fine," I said. I swallowed hard then, and keeping my voice as neutral as possible, addressed Nate. "How come you're driving us to school? Are you on reading break from BU right now?"

I knew I was making an idiot of myself, that the Casey from this realm would know the answer to these questions, but I didn't care. I didn't plan on sticking around here for long anyway. As soon as I could manage to trigger it, I was hopefully back to 1929 and undoing whatever it was I'd done.

I just wanted to know how there could be a world where it was possible that Nate was with Lucinda and not me. Where he could be doing anything besides going to Boston University and be halfway through his degree?

Lucinda didn't let him answer. "Why would he be at BU, Case? You know he has to work for a couple more years to save money to go."

Nate didn't get his scholarship?

Lucinda smiled widely at him and placed a slender hand on his shoulder. "We'll get to go together, so it's perfect, actually."

I threw up a little in my mouth. "Right," I mumbled. "Of course."

Nate pulled up in the student parking lot of Cambridge High. When they leaned into each other for the inevitable good-bye kiss, I scrambled out the back and kept walking. There was no way I was watching *that!*

I'd disappeared into the crowd of students before Lucinda could call after me. I went to my locker and spun the dial by memory. I'd had the same combination lock since my freshman year and could unlock it with my eyes closed and my hands tied behind my back.

Except this time it wouldn't click open. I tried a second and third time, saying the numbers out loud and it wouldn't budge.

Man! What more could go wrong? So humiliating to have to go to the office at the end of my senior year because I couldn't get my locker open!

"What are you doing?"

I turned to a familiar voice. Artimisha Hilbert from my notorious Hollywood school trip. "Misha?"

"What you doing with my lock?"

I glanced down at the metal contraption in my palm. Was this Misha's locker? Then where was mine?

"Oh? I um…"

"You traded with me, remember? So you could be next to *Austin King.*" She said Austin's name like she was spitting out venom.

"Right, just habit," I said, backing away. "I wasn't thinking."

I must've gotten together with Austin in Hollywood. What a mess! I had to get to the library and find out what the heck happened with Lolly to create this.

I headed in the direction of Austin King's locker and braced myself for whatever reaction I was about to get from him. Thankfully, he wasn't there and I only had to try the lock on either side of his to find the one that opened for me. I had no idea what class I had, but since I was heading for the library, it didn't matter. My locker was organized the same way as in my own world. There was something comforting in knowing that at my core, I stayed the same person, no matter what the circumstances were around me.

I tossed my backpack inside and grabbed a notebook and pen. Before I could secure my locker closed, someone grabbed me by the waist from behind and swung me around. I let out a little scream and then another when a set of lips nibbled on my neck.

"Hey," Austin said, as he put me down. "Jumpy much?"

"Oh, yeah, I'm…"

"What happened to you yesterday anyway?" Blond hair fell into his eyes and he swept it to the side. "We were supposed to go out, but your mom told me you were sick? But not so sick Lucinda and her tag-along couldn't see you?" I wasn't sure if he was sincerely hurt or just a little controlling.

"I know, I can explain. I think I ate something off and I was just out of it." Excuse as to why I couldn't see

45

him. Now something to cover Lucinda. "I needed to borrow notes from Lucinda, so she brought them over."

He seemed to accept that and threaded his fingers through mine. I threw my shoulders back, deciding I better play the part. Anything else would cause undue attention and I was already getting enough of that.

Austin kept a firm clasp of my hand as we navigated down the halls. I'd just have to see where he dropped me off, since he must know where he was taking me, and as soon as he was out of sight, I'd sneak off to the library.

I spotted Tim coming toward us. He sauntered confidently like a proud peacock, arm draped around Jessica Fuller's shoulder. I swallowed sourly. He was younger than her by a year, but by the gushing glow on her face as she stared up at him, she didn't care. He joked around with a couple other jocks as they walked past. One of them announced the party spot for the weekend, and Tim nodded.

He and Jessica stopped by the open door of a classroom and Tim pressed her up against the lockers and laid a good one on her. Who was this guy? Certainly not my brother!

She giggled before disappearing into the classroom and Tim resumed his jock-man stride. When he saw Austin and me, he gave a little chin-nod of acknowledgement.

I had no doubt that Austin wouldn't let Tim show him up in the kiss-your-girlfriend-goodbye ritual and my mind swam as I tried to come up with a plausible reason not to kiss Austin.

Cold sore forming? Thrush? Toothache?

I was so frantic to come up with a plan, before I knew it we were both in the same classroom and Austin claimed one of the desks. He looked at me like he was waiting for me to sit at the desk beside him. Mr. Ryerson stood at the front of the class and I realized with disappointment that I was in my creative writing class. I reluctantly sat. My search for answers at the library would have to wait.

Chapter Six

I pretended to read the book Ryerson had handed out, but right now I could care less about this class or any assignment. The words blurred before me as my mind scrambled to work out a plan. I'd run to the library as soon as the bell rang, hide myself until the next class started, then slip into one of the computer booths and not leave until I figured out what had happened.

"You actually have to turn the pages once in awhile."

I snapped up at Austin's whispering voice. He frowned at me and I turned back to my open book, and flicked over a page.

What if I didn't get back to my real timeline? What if I were stuck here? I'd probably have to eventually pay attention in this class, and the others. I'd have to watch Lucinda's relationship with Nate grow.

I shuddered. I had to get back to my own time!

The bell rang and the room erupted with chatter, the scraping of chairs along the vinyl flooring, and dragging footsteps. I quickly headed out behind the crowd.

Austin grabbed my arm and pulled me free of the throng of bodies easing down the hallway.

"What's wrong with you Casey? You're acting like a loon!"

"I'm sorry. I can't explain… I just have to go."

"Do you want to break up with me already? Is that it? Because I'm cool with that. Just don't lead me on."

I locked on to his serious blue-eyed stare and felt a flutter of remorse. I never wanted to hurt Austin, not in any timeline. "Yes," I said, honestly. "I'm sorry, but I can't do this with you anymore."

Austin took a sharp step backward, palms up. His eyes shuttered with pain and he shook his head. "Fine," he said. "Have it your way."

I shoved back all the volcanic emotions in my chest, put my chin down and headed straight for the library. I spotted Tim. He bumped a skinny guy into the lockers as he passed him in the hall. His gang of jocks laughed at the poor guy's expense.

Great, my brother was a jerk and a bully.

I finally made it into the library and found a spot out of the librarian's direct line of vision. It felt like an eternity since I had left the house this morning with this destination in mind.

49

I logged into my student account, letting out a small breath of relief that I got in so easily and googled the Kavanaugh family of Cambridge. I found the family tree and a short history.

Kavanaugh, Dougal and Annie: until 1936 owned a farm at Warren Lane (currently the site of West Gate Subdivision, Cambridge). Forced to sell during the Great Depression due to financial difficulties. One daughter, Lolita; married Mulligan, Brian (1931).

I was confused. There was nothing scandalous about Lolly that would cause such a revised timeline. Was she supposed to actually marry Thomas Burgess? Had she married him, would they have been able to save the farm? Would that have made the difference?

Now I felt bad for discouraging her toward Thomas. When was I going to learn to keep my nose out of things that weren't my business!

I had to get back and convince her that Thomas was the one for her. Talk her out of her "modern woman" movement, though I was saddened by that part. Apparently, Lolly's contribution to the feminist movement had never been meant to be a large one, which was fine by me if it meant getting back to my own time.

I'd figured out that my school schedules were the same, and my time spent in the library was time spent missing field hockey. It was one of my better sports because the stick did provide a measure of distance from the opposing players, though some of the girls played rough and liked to body check. Because of that, I had to wear long sleeves, no matter how hot it was outside.

Everyone, at least in my own realm, was aware of my "arm fetish" and no longer paid any heed to it.

There was a tense moment in the hallway when Austin and I both turned a corner from opposite directions and nearly plowed into each other. He glared at me and I mumbled another apology under my breath.

Lucinda met me at my locker after the last class, and I was grateful for the day to end and to get a ride home. I secretly longed to see Nate again, even if it was from my view from the back seat. There I could gaze at his profile without Lucinda noticing. I loved Nate's face, his dark lashes, his stately nose and the bristle that covered his jaw. I couldn't run my fingers along his cheeks anymore, but I could stare. I could indulge in sweet eye candy.

Lucinda popped my bubble. "Do you think you could catch a ride home with Tim?"

"W-why?" I stammered. I didn't want Tim. I wanted Nate!

Lucinda's bronze cheeks blushed crimson. "It's Friday and Nate has plans."

"Plans?" I squeaked out.

Lucinda leaned in. "Special plans. I think he's going to ask me to the prom."

What!!!

"It's only three and a half weeks away, so it's about time!" She giggled. "We can double date with you and Austin."

I groaned. I totally forgot about the prom. Why had I jumped the gun with Austin? If I was stuck in this timeline, I'd rather have a date then go to the prom solo. I was already such a loser.

"Casey?" Lucinda said kindly. "Are you going to tell me what's going on? Is everything all right with you and Austin?"

Right! Austin could be the scapegoat to explain my manic behavior. I shook my head, "No. We broke up." It was easy to summon the tears to support my case. A true-to-life nervous breakdown was just around the corner anyway.

"Oh, Casey. I'm so sorry. I've been too busy with Nate to notice things had gotten bad with you and Austin." She stared up into my watery eyes. "You guys hid it really well. No one would've guessed you two weren't madly in love."

Did I love Austin King? Was it possible that in another timeline, this timeline, I actually loved Austin the way I had loved Nate?

"Well," I started, busying myself in my locker so I wouldn't have to look at her, "it's a confusing time."

"I wish I could stay with you, but I promised Nate."

"It's fine. I'll catch a ride with Tim." I should've said something cute, like "have fun" or "don't do anything I wouldn't do," but I couldn't bring myself to cheer her on.

"I'll call you," she said.

"Okay."

I found Tim in the parking lot. To my dismay, Jessica Fuller with her perfectly coiffed "strawberry blond" hair, was sliding into the front seat.

"Tim!" I shouted before he could take off without me. "I need a ride."

"Where's Lucinda's chauffeur?" he asked snidely. I ignored him and jumped in the back seat of his Corolla.

Jessica cast me a wry glance but didn't say anything in greeting. Once we were on the road, she bothered to ask me about the prom.

"Have you picked out your dress yet? What color are you and Austin sharing?"

"Color sharing?" I returned.

"You know, his cummerbund and your dress. Have you picked a color?"

I shook my head.

"We have, Timmy, right?" She smiled at my brother in a way that made me want to gag. Then she spun around to stare back at me. "We're going with emerald green."

"Wasn't that the color you wore at the Fall Dance in our sophomore year?" I asked, not so kindly. That was the year she had taunted me with her popularity and paraded around with Nate on her arm. She'd laughed at me when we ran into each other at Filenes and I knocked over a rack of dresses.

"*No*," she said sourly. "I wore yellow. Saffron, actually."

No, she didn't. *I* wore saffron! This new reality was driving me crazy!

53

Tim skidded into the driveway of our house and gave me a look that said, "Get out." I assumed he was driving Jessica home and would be busy the rest of the night. I was probably the only senior at Cambridge High that was staying home on a Friday night.

The house was quiet and empty and I was glad. I didn't think I could pretend everything was okay with either of my parents. I just needed time to have a personal meltdown in the privacy of my own room.

I took a moment to grab a bowl of Cheerios and carried it with me upstairs. I slurped the sugary milk as my mind tried to figure out this next riddle. Every other time I needed to manufacture a tripping episode I always had either Lucinda or Nate (or both) to help me figure out a way. This was the first time I was forced to manage on my own. Something that made me stress—as if I hadn't had enough stress already! Why hadn't I tripped by now? Oh please, I wasn't really stuck here, was I?

My phone chirped and I jumped. I'd forgotten I even had a phone here and was more surprised by the fact that it worked. Obviously Nate wouldn't be texting me, so it must be Lucinda.

I glanced at the screen. Or Austin. I choked on my cereal when I read his text.

Austin: I love you. And I know you love me, too. I don't know what happened to you yesterday but you can talk to me. You know that, right? I'm here for you. <3

I dropped my spoon and milk flicked all over my shirt.

The me from here loved Austin. I had to make things right so that when I left, things would unfold as they were meant to in this timeline.

I couldn't bring myself to confess a love I didn't feel, but I put out a white flag.

Casey: I'm sorry. I don't actually want to break up. Forgive me?

Austin: Of course! You don't know how happy I am to hear that! Can I come over?

It was one thing to play along via text, but I just couldn't do it in person.

Casey: I know it's Friday, but I'm really not feeling well. I want to see you, but I don't want you to catch this bug. :)

Austin: See? You do love me! Okay, I'll hang with the guys. I'll come by tomorrow.

Casey: Okay.

I had to be gone by tomorrow. *Think, Casey!* What could I do to prompt a trip back to Lolly's farm?

I could go see Nate. That would do it for sure. The perk would be I'd arrive at Lolly's farm when I tripped and save myself a big walk.

First I needed to visit the costume shop, so I'd arrive prepared this time.

I caught the bus and easily found the costume shop. None of the structures had changed in this timeline, it seemed: just people and the relationships between some of them. I carefully chose the best two twenties-era dresses I could find, a fancy one and a simple one, along with the strap-and-buckle, two-inch square-heeled shoes that were in style then and a pair of thick stockings. I'd be fine without accessories and makeup: Lolly and Marlene had always been quick to share theirs, and besides, my cosmetic contributions from this era wouldn't fit in with that one.

I called Mom and told her I'd be out with friends and not to wait up for me. Instead, I caught the bus and wandered the mall. I bought a noodle bowl at the food court and practice using chopsticks just to pass the time. I remembered being here, in a different time with Willie Watson, whom I'd accidentally brought home from the past. Thinking of him and my time with the Watsons in 1863 made me feel happy and sad at the same time.

I browsed through the clothing shops and ducked behind a group of skinny mannequins when I saw a couple of girls who were friends with Jessica Fuller. I didn't want to be called out for being alone or weird. Weirder.

I strolled past the clock shop where I had bought Nate's pocket watch, my failed "big gesture" and paused to view the old man tinkering with something behind the counter. I didn't go in. My heart couldn't bear it.

Finally, the mall shops began to close and I caught a late bus to the stop on Nate's street. I knew I was about to make a fool of myself, but I couldn't stand knowing there was a timeline where Nate and I weren't together. I had to tell him how I felt. Maybe it would translate through the cosmos somehow and *my* Nate would know that I loved him and that it was so wrong for us not to be together.

There was a swing on the Mackenzie porch and I padded quietly to it and sat down. The lamplight was out and a huge hydrangea bush obscured the street view. I propped my backpack beside me and waited.

Crickets hummed loudly and a warm early summer breeze carried the spring floral scent. If my stomach hadn't been in a massive knot, it would've been really relaxing.

It was well past midnight when headlights turned up the drive. I heard one door open and then slam shut. Good, that meant he was alone.

My heart thundered as his silhouette climbed the steps. His keys jangled as he slipped one into the lock. My throat was caught on a dry swallow and if I didn't speak up, Nate would soon disappear inside.

"Hey," I mustered.

Nate jumped.

"It's me, Casey," I said quickly. "Sorry. I didn't mean to scare you."

Nate pressed his hands against his chest. "What are you doing here?"

"I uh…" Now that I was here standing face to face with Nate, I had serious second thoughts about what I was about to do.

"Casey?"

"I'm in love with you, Nate!" I blurted. "You're the only one for me, ever."

He rattled his head like he was trying to knock water out of his ears. "What?"

"I love you. And you love me. Our love transcends time..."

He took a step back and held out a palm. "Whoa...."

I bit my lip. I'd waxed eloquent and instead of sounding inspired and romantic, it sounded silly and desperate.

"I don't know what's going on with you Casey, but Lucinda's your best friend. How could you say that to me? How could you do something like this to her?"

"It's hard to explain..." Oh, this was so not turning out how I'd imagined! Which was what exactly, anyway? Had I expected him to say, "Hey, you're right. Deep down in my gut I felt it all along. I just needed you to point it out"?

My face burned with embarrassment and I was thankful for the darkness of night.

"Lucinda told me that you and Austin have been having troubles. You're just confused." He cocked his head. "Have you been drinking?"

"No!" I wasn't confused. Just incredibly stupid!

He sighed. "I know Lucinda wanted to tell you, but I think, with this, you should probably know now."

"Know what?" I braced myself for the worst, but nothing could have prepared me for what he said next.

"I asked Lucinda to marry me."

Elle Strauss

Chapter Seven

This couldn t be happening. *No, no, no, no!* Nate and Lucinda were not supposed to get married!

Blood rushed to my cheeks making them feel heavy like sandbags, and my eyes burned with hot tears of mortification. I stumbled down Nate's drive to the road like the drunk he had accused me of being. There was enough light from the street lamps that I could make my way in the darkness, even with blurry vision.

I let out a loud hiccup of humiliation. Man, I hated this timeline! If I was still here tomorrow, I'd have to face Lucinda (and Nate!) and live through all their happy couple talk, pretending like it wasn't just *killing* me.

A car honked from behind me and I jumped out of my skin, almost falling into the ditch. It slowly rolled by and the driver and passenger, both guys, eyed me with interest.

And not in a good way. The passenger nodded and tipped a beer can in salute.

Great. They were drinking.

I was stupid to be walking home in the dark in the middle of the night. Even with taking the bus, it wasn't cool to go solo. I wrapped my arms around my chest and stared straight ahead.

My Nate would never have let me walk home alone at this time of night and not just because I was his girlfriend. He wouldn't have let any girl do it. I really must've messed up his head with my declaration.

The car almost disappeared in the distance and I thought I was in the clear until it slowed and turned around. Oh no. They were coming back!

My mind raced. What should I do? Nate's neighborhood wasn't the crowded kind. His house was on a big lot and set in a good distance from the road. It would be a good jog to the front door of the nearest house, and unfortunately all the lights there were out. I'd have to ring the bell and knock and hope that someone was home and didn't mind being woken up.

I broke into a jog, hoping to make it to the driveway entrance before the car reached it. It was like they knew what I was going to do and sped up. I ran. The headlights bore down on me. I could judge the distance to the driveway and their speed of approach. I wasn't going to make it. Their headlights blinded me. I screamed.

Suddenly, everything was gone. The houses, the car, the two guys in the front seat. I doubled over, clutching my chest, trying to catch my breath. I'd tripped to the past and not a second too soon.

At least I still had my backpack. If I'd thought enough to drop it, I probably would've made it to the driveway, but I was in a panic and didn't think. I likely wouldn't have made it to the front door anyway. I was just glad to be out of that situation and to have my costumes with me.

I was in the middle of Lolly's field. The moonlight highlighted her small house in the distance, a shadowy two-story structure. They didn't have electricity. Even though Boston main was thoroughly lit up, many of the farms still relied on oil lamps and wood stoves. I walked between the rows of carrots and other vegetables, and when I reached the house, I carefully climbed onto a half-empty rain barrel and pulled myself up onto the gable. I inched my way around the slanted roof until I came to Lolly's window.

Tap, tap, tap. I knocked lightly, not wanting to inadvertently wake up Mr. and Mrs. Kavanaugh. Especially Mrs. Kavanaugh. She was a no-nonsense woman and wouldn't put up with my sort of shenanigans. I was amazed Lolly got away with what she did running into town to hang out with city girls.

I tapped the glass again.

A pale hand moved the lace curtain from the window and I saw Lolly gasp and jump back.

"Lolly," I said with a low urgency. "It's just me. Casey."

Lolly worked the stiff window open and stepped away so I could swing my legs over the wooden sill and slide in.

She wore a long, cream-colored nightgown, and tiptoed across her wooden floors in bare feet. She picked up a ladder-back chair and tucked it under the door handle.

"For crying out loud!"

I put a finger to my lips. "You don't want to wake up your parents."

She lowered her voice to a whisper. "What the futz, Casey. Where are your parents? Do they know you're traipsing around in the middle of the night dressed like a waif?"

"No, they don't know, and I can't tell them." I put on my best "trust me" face. "I'll explain everything in the morning. Can I please just sleep here?"

Her face softened. "Is someone not treating you right?"

I offered a subtle shrug. Right now I'd let her believe whatever she wanted if it meant I could stay here until morning. When I thought of what could've happened to me with those guys...I started trembling.

Lolly noticed. "Oh, darlin'. Yes, you can stay." She opened a dresser drawer and offered me one of her granny gowns. "Here you go. The mattress is big enough for the both of us if we lay straight."

"Thank you," I said.

I turned my back to her as I worked myself out of my skinny jeans and T-shirt, and pulled the nighty over my head. Lolly crawled into bed, shaking her head at me. "I'm not going to pretend to understand why you wear such horribly inappropriate clothes."

I wanted to wash my face and use the washroom, but I knew all about the outhouse. This farm still depended on a well for its water supply. I'd used the restroom at the mall several hours ago, and though I wouldn't have minded a chance to relieve myself, I was determined to hold it.

I slipped under the covers next to Lolly, flat on my back as close to the edge as I could without falling off, leaving a good six inches between us.

Nate had thought Marlene and her mother would be my new family, but I was beginning to think it was the Kavanaughs. The location of Lolly's farm was a short bus ride from my house when I tripped back. I could avoid Boston, just make myself useful on the farm. Lolly wasn't interested in farming, but I didn't mind. Anything to stay out of trouble while keeping my stomach filled and a safe place to sleep was fine with me. I just had to work on getting on Mrs. Kavanaugh's good side.

Lolly's breathing settled into an easy rhythm as she fell asleep. I was still too worked up to follow suit, my mind all over the place. Nate's rejection (again!), the guys who came after me, the fact that I was back in 1929 with the monumental task of resetting the timeline back to what it was. My chest felt like it was about to cave in.

Nate's big announcement. It troubled me, but not just because there was a timeline where Nate would propose to Lucinda, but because in my own timeline, even before my Hollywood screw-up, Nate hadn't mentioned anything about marriage.

Sure, I think we both assumed it would happen eventually, because once upon a time, we were both committed to going the distance.

What changed that? The kiss I shared with Austin?

I had to believe that there was something else going on before my misstep. As awful as it was, it was just a kiss. Nothing so formidable that Nate and I couldn't get past it if we both wanted to.

I had to face that fact that, even if Nate wasn't into Fiona, he'd still been growing away from me.

Deep down I had known this would happen. How many high school relationships actually go on to be long happy marriages? Not many. I had thought Nate and I were special because we shared something so unique—my ability to travel through time. How crazy for me to think that something like that would be a binding agent!

Which made me wonder: would Nate ever have loved me if I hadn't been a traveler? If he hadn't developed a sense of responsibility for me?

The answer was a resounding *no*. He never would've noticed me if it weren't for that first accidental trip.

Our relationship had always been a ticking bomb. If it hadn't been Spain/Fiona and Hollywood/Austin, it would've been something else eventually.

This line of thought was *not* helping me get to sleep.

Chapter Eight

Loud knocking was followed by a bellow. "Lolita! You open this door this minute!"

My eyes snapped open and my heart thudded in my ears as awareness of my situation returned. I was camped out in Lolly Kavanaugh's room in 1929, and her irate mother was pounding on the bedroom door.

I blinked through my brain fog. Dawn had just been breaking when I'd finally drifted off to sleep and it didn't look that much lighter out. I maybe got three hours of sleep.

Lolly nudged my shoulder and whispered into my ear. "Get under the bed."

"What?"

"Under the bed! Ma can't find you here."

I didn't understand why, but I did what I was told. The bed frame scraped along my back as I scooted underneath, and the dust bunnies made my nose itch. I pinched it to ward off a sneeze.

"Coming Ma," Lolly called.

"Do you have someone in here?" Mrs. Kavanaugh's footsteps snapped against the floor as she crossed the room. I froze. How was I going to explain hiding under Lolly's bed? I could see her brown lace-up shoes as she paused by the window.

"What are you looking for?" Lolly said. "There's no one here."

"Sally Brown caught her daughter sneaking out with a boy. That kind of shameless behaviour was unheard of in my day!"

"I'm not sneaking out with anyone."

"So why do you have the chair under your door?"

Lolly spoke boldly. "To keep you out, Ma."

"Lolita!"

"Ma! A girl needs some privacy. Now let me get dressed, so I can go tend to the chickens."

Mrs. Kavanaugh's quick footsteps faded as Lolly closed the bedroom door. I was too nervous to move. What if Mrs. Kavanaugh came back?

Lolly bent down and stared at me under the bed. A mischievous smile crossed her face. "Are you going to stay under there all day?"

"Maybe. If you have a bed pan."

"All out of bed pans, but I for one am eager to heed nature's call."

68

I shimmied out from under the bed and brushed the house dust from the nighty I wore. "What am I supposed to do?" I obviously couldn't follow Lolly downstairs.

Lolly tossed me some work clothes. "Put these on. Sneak out the window and come to the kitchen door and ask to see me."

"And when your mother asks why I want to see you?"

Lolly shrugged. "I'm sure you have a good story made up already. Use that." She disappeared out of the bedroom just as Mrs. Kavanaugh bellowed her name up the stairwell.

"Coming, Ma!"

I changed clothes and used a ribbon I found on Lolly's dresser to tie back my hair. The problem was, I didn't have a good story. I had to come up with something, but first I just *had* to visit the outhouse.

I was used to such things from hanging out at the Watsons, so I went inside the stall, held my breath and did my business. I stared blankly at the iconic sliver moon cut out for light. I needed a story.

When I thought I'd come up with a plausible one, I started toward the house as instructed by Lolly. I came around the corner just as Mr. Kavanaugh swung around the opposite side. He stopped short when he saw me.

I called out, "Hello, Mr. Kavanaugh. It's Casey. I was here for dinner the other night."

He furrowed a brow like he had no recollection at all. Maybe he couldn't place me because of how I was now dressed. He nodded politely and entered the house without a word. It didn't surprise me that Mr. Kavanaugh wasn't a big talker. Mrs. Kavanaugh filled up all the space for that.

I stayed outside and rapped on the open door. Even though I'd been a guest previously, it didn't feel right for me to just walk in. Mrs. Kavanaugh's frame filled the doorway and she eyed me suspiciously. "You selling somethin'? Cuz we don't need nothin'."

"No, Mrs. Kavanaugh. It's Casey, Lolly's friend? I was here for dinner the other night."

She scowled. "I remember you. Ran off without a word of explanation. What'd ya want?"

"Is Lolly home?"

"What'd you want her for?"

Now for the story. "Well, I'm working for the Burgess farm…"

"Thomas Burgess's family?"

"That's right. We need an extra hand, and they sent me to ask if Lolly was available?"

"Is that right?"

I thought I saw an upward twitch to her mouth. "Lolly would be pleased to go. Arthur and I can manage for one day. But first, come in for breakfast."

She waved me in, and I didn't argue. You could smell bacon frying from a mile a way and my mouth was already watering.

Lolly entered with a basket of eggs, her eyes widening at the sight of her mother and me in the kitchen.

"Casey is Burgess's new hire," her mom explained. "They need your help and of course, we'll help." She pierced Lolly with a glare that said, "Don't you dare mess with me." Her shoulders were back like she was expecting a challenge. Lolly glanced at me briefly and I caught the imperceptive twinkle in her eye.

"If it means getting out from under your eagle eye for a day, Ma…"

"Don't you lip me."

"I'm just teasing. Oh, I wonder what Thomas has in store for me today?"

Mrs. Kavanaugh's eyes widened in alarm, and Lolly burst out laughing. I almost felt sorry for Mrs. Kavanaugh. It seemed she met her match in her daughter when it came to strong personalities.

I just hoped Lolly wasn't too strong. I needed to change her mind about Thomas somehow, and quickly.

Breakfast wasn't the fancy affair that dinner had been, and I had the distinct impression most meals around here weren't fancy, and if it hadn't been for Mrs. Kavanaugh's efforts to woo Thomas Burgess on behalf of her daughter, the other dinner wouldn't have been either. My sudden departure probably hadn't helped matters when it came to managing pleasantries and nudging Lolly and Thomas together. Now was as good a time as any to try to make up for it.

"Thomas Burgess is a great boss," I said. "And in favor of equal opportunities. Treats women the same as men."

Lolly froze, a well-buttered piece of toast in her mouth. She couldn't talk but she sent me a message with her eyes. *What are you doing?*

I wasn't sure. I hoped I was sowing seeds, no pun intended, to convince her to reconsider farming.

She swallowed then challenged me. "How long have you been working for the Burgess's exactly?"

I blinked, aware that I was being carefully watched by the whole Kavanaugh family. "Not long, but I can tell already that Thomas is a good guy."

"A good *guy*?"

Oops. I was screwing up the vernacular of the day. "Fella, I mean. He's a good fella."

Lolly cocked a brow. "Is that right?"

I wasn't about to back down. She might have a strong personality, but I was no pushover, either. "Uh-huh. And farming is honorable work. Someone has to produce the food to feed the nation. He should get a medal."

Lolly glared at me, clearly unimpressed by my traitorous words.

Mrs. K put down her coffee mug. "You never did say where your own farm is located, Casey."

No, I didn't.

"It's not near here, and well, it's not doing well. It's why I've had to find work elsewhere."

"And you're not interested in being a secretary," she said with a glance at Lolly. "I heard it's what all the modern girls are doing."

"I'm happy to work on the farm, ma'am. Work is work, and if you can call your own shots from home, rather than working for a man in a slick suit who wants who knows what…"

Mrs. Kavanaugh slapped the table with enthusiasm."That's exactly what I tell my Lolita!"

Points for me! Getting Mrs. Kavanaugh on my side is part of Plan "Adopt a New Family." Now to achieve Plan "Reset Timeline to Normal."

When I faced Lolly, her eyes were steely slits of anger. Negative points for Plan Reset. She picked up her empty plate. "We should get going. Don't want to keep Good Fella Thomas Burgess waiting."

I sighed and tossed Mrs. Kavanaugh an apologetic look. I'd over-stated my case concerning Thomas Burgess and had made us both unhappy.

Chapter Nine

Lolly stormed to the garage where the car was kept and slammed the driver's door after she slid inside. She watched me coolly until I was sitting beside her, then backed out of the garage, drove out onto the dirt road and shifted the car into a higher gear. Dust sputtered up behind us on the dirt road.

She finally spoke up "Jeepers creepers, Casey! What was that all about?"

I played stupid. "What?"

"*Thomas Burgess is a good fella,*" she mimicked.

"Well, isn't he? Besides the fact that you don't want to join farms, is there anything wrong with him? He looked nice to me."

"Then you marry him!"

Lolly pulled to the side of the road once the Kavanaugh farm was out of sight. She'd tossed a burlap bag and my backpack in the backseat sometime before the now infamous breakfast. She handed me the backpack, then reached for her bag and pulled out a dress and dress shoes. She closed herself into the backseat and began the awkward task of changing clothes. I did the same in the front seat with the costume in my backpack.

"It's just," I said as I pushed my head through the neck hole of my dress, "that sometimes you have to look at the bigger picture. Step back a little and see what is the best move for everyone. Joining farms would help your parents so much, and I'm sure the Burgess' would benefit, too."

"I don't love him."

"Love is a two-edged sword," I said with more spite in my voice than I intended. "It's the best feeling in the world until it's the worst feeling in the world. Trust me. You can live without it."

"Is this about your fella?" Her expression softened. "Did he break it off for good? Was that why you were crying last night?"

Tears pricked the back of my eyes and I looked away.

Lolly hopped back into the driver's side and checked her face in the mirror before flashing me her bright smile. "Let's not think about fellas or farming today, huh? Life's too short. Let's dive into Marlene's makeup bag and then go have us a fun day!"

Marlene looked like she'd had more fun than she could manage. She answered the door in a silky nightgown, but that was the only point of glamour. Her eyes were puffy and bloodshot and her hair a tossed mess. The house was completely littered with empty glasses, bottles and overflowing ashtrays. One of the red ladder chairs had a broken back.

"Come in!" Marlene said, pulling on Lolly's arm. "You scared me to death. I thought you were the coppers. I didn't know you were coming today."

"Clearly," I said under my breath. Mrs. Charter was going to have a fit when she got home.

"I need your help. I have to meet Ma at the train station at eight tonight." Marlene's eyes darted frantically at the disaster. "Oh, rhatz! What am I going to do?"

I wasn't a partier in my own time, but despite heavy objections from me, Tim had thrown a couple doozies when our parents had been out of town. I had experience cleaning up after one.

"Do you have garbage bags? Or empty boxes?" I said, taking charge. "Let's get rid of the empties first."

"Don't know whatcha mean by garbage bags," Marlene said, "but I got cardboard boxes." Marlene disappeared for a couple minutes and returned with the boxes and we began the collection. Marlene's stance seemed to soften toward me. Maybe because she appreciated my help. Or maybe she was just tired from her wild night.

"How did this happen, Marlene?" Lolly said. "I thought Sheldon was here to manage things?"

I cut a look to Marlene, curious about her response. Her back stiffened and her expression shuttered close.

"He left when the police came."

"The police were here?" I waved at the mess. "And then what?"

"They never came inside. I sweet-talked them, telling them it was an all girls party, and that their wives would blush if they came inside. I promised to keep the noise down."

I grinned with admiration. "Quick thinking."

We washed the glasses and ashtrays and wiped down the tables and kitchen counters. Marlene's family owned a vacuum cleaner—only the wealthy had those—which was a big help to our efforts, though this one felt like a steel tank. My arms burned as I pushed it along the carpet area.

Lolly leaned over the sofa, staring hard at something on the seat. "Oh no," she said. "A cigarette burn!"

Marlene scampered over to her. "Where?"

Lolly pointed to a small, but noticeable blemish. I picked up the cushion and turned it over. "There." That was an easy fix, but the broken chair was another matter.

"I can get another one at the hardware store," Marlene said. "Lolly, I'll give you money. Can you go pick it up? I'm not ready to face the public."

Lolly huffed, and pointed to her head. "I can't go out with this face."

We hadn't had time to "dive" into Marlene's cosmetics yet.

"I'll do it," I offered. I didn't care about my face.

Marlene padded my palm with a wad of bills. "You're swell, Casey. I owe ya."

That was good news to me, because I was certain that I'd have to cash in on that promise some day.

I liked the Boston of 1929. It was more modern and sophisticated than the 1860s version, yet not as cluttered and populated as the present. The streets were lined with buildings made of fiery-red brick and trimmed with black shutters around the windows and black wrought iron railings along the steps. The neighborhood glowed warmly in the late morning sun.

Pete's Hardware took up a corner lot one block away. A little bell rang over the door as I entered, and a robust man stocking one of the shelves greeted me.

"Good morning! Welcome to Pete's. I'm Pete. How can I be of service?"

"I heard that you stock wooden ladder-back chairs?"

"I do. There are a couple in the back. Follow me."

He whistled while meandering down the aisle. He caught the eyes of other customers and they exchanged smiles. This neighborhood was still small enough that everyone knew each other. It would explain their cautious stances toward me.

I recognized one dark head: it was Paul Junior from the speakeasy. He stared at me with interest. I held out a finger, and mouthed, "Wait for me."

"There you go, miss." Pete pointed to several chairs lined up against a wall. Thankfully one of them was red.

"I'll take that one," I said. He nodded gleefully and scooped up my selection. "It'll be waiting for you at the checkout. Can I help you with anything else?"

I shook my head. "I'm just going to have a look around. Thanks."

I headed back to where I'd spotted Paul Junior and prayed he'd stuck around. I smiled when I saw him bending low in one of the aisles, checking out a metal bucket.

"Roland says we need a new one," he said without looking up at me

"You can't have too many buckets."

He scratched the back of his head and then stared up at me. "Where'd you go the other day?"

"Let's talk about it outside," I said. I paid for Marlene's chair and Paul Junior paid for the bucket. He insisted on carrying the chair back to Marlene's for me. I took his bucket.

We walked side by side in silence as I tried to work out where to begin. What had Paul Junior seen? And more importantly, what did he think he'd seen?

He braced the chair on one hip, keeping his eyes on the sidewalk. Dark tufts of hair wafted over a somber face.

"Where'd you go then?" he asked again.

"What do you mean?"

"You ran into the kitchen and then 'poof' you were gone. Like magic."

Like magic? Was that what he really thought?

"I didn't disappear like magic," I said carefully. "I simply turned around and went back into the bar. Quick like. While you were blinking."

Paul Junior cast a curious glance my way. "Then why didn't you come back into the kitchen? Finish the night out?"

"Something came up. Something I just had to attend to. I'm so sorry for leaving you with all the clean-up."

"Uh-huh," he said, but he didn't sound convinced.

I wasn't exactly convinced either. "What about you?" I probed cautiously. "Do you sometimes disappear like magic?"

We'd arrived at the front of Marlene's brownstone. Paul Junior carried the chair to the top of the steps and set it down in front of the door. Then he reached for my pail while answering my question belatedly. "I suppose I do."

He skipped down the steps and down the sidewalk, metal pail swinging from his skinny arm.

I turn to the door, not sure if I should just go in or knock. I wasn't family or a close friend, but I *was* helping Marlene out of a crisis.

Just as I put my hand on the knob, another one slapped on top of it. Paul Junior had returned and he had a crazed look in his eye.

I screamed as we tumbled together into the light.

Chapter Ten

"Paul Junior! Are you crazy?"

I knew where we were. I knew *when* we were. I just couldn't fathom why. This wasn't accidental. He'd done this on purpose. A hijacking of a colossal kind.

Paul Junior looked embarrassed, like he couldn't believe what he'd done either.

"I'm sorry, Casey. I knew you'd understand, and I really need your help."

"You knew I'd understand?? How did you know that?"

"Because, I saw that you were like me. You disappeared…"

We stood in the streets of old Boston. Way older than I'd ever seen before.

"1775?" I asked to confirm. Paul Junior just nodded his head. The brownstones from 1929 were gone, replaced by single-story wooden homes, knotted together in rows. The wide streets weren't cobbled, just hard mud with distressingly deep potholes, and they were crowded with pedestrians. The men were dressed in layered shades of brown, and wore three-cornered hats over long hair tied back in ponytails.

Unless they were service men in the British army. The soldiers wore handsome red coats with black lapels, wide white ornate edging and brass buttons, and tight white pants that looked like riding dungarees, tucked into knee-high leather boots. They had on ridiculous-looking white wigs under their hats that had two or three horizontal ring-curls over each ear and a black bow tying the fake ponytail.

The women on the street were dressed in large, full skirts and many wore what looked like night caps on their heads. A rickety carriage pushed its way through the throng, horse neighing and rider shouting at the people to get out of the way. From what I could see through the small windows, the passengers were dressed nothing like the onlookers in the streets. They wore colourful shiny clothes, the man with a tight frilly collar and a fancy gray wig, his female companion with a wig high enough to touch the ceiling of the carriage and the tight bodice of her dress pushing her breasts up like buns rising in a pan.

I, on the other hand, was dressed primed to be burned at the stake.

Paul looked me up and down, obviously sharing my concern. He waved for me to follow him down a shadowy, narrow alley.

"I'll fetch a dress from my sister," he said.

I was thankful that most people I encountered as I tripped into the past had sisters. I wore a lot of their clothing.

Now that I'd noticed them, there seemed to be a lot of red coats—which made sense because this was the time of the British occupation of Boston.

I was so busy watching the back of Paul Junior's head and the uneven ground beneath my feet that I hadn't even noticed where we were going. I shouldn't have been surprise to have arrived at an early version of the Paul Revere house—which was a museum in both my own time and 1929.

It was odd to see it so small, as it was before Paul Revere Senior had the addition built and sitting a comfortable distance from its neighbors. In my time, Boston had grown up around the house, smothering and dwarfing it as it had other old landmarks.

Paul Junior pointed to a weather-worn shed nearly hidden from view by a runaway lilac bush. "Wait here," he said before disappearing.

Alone behind the Paul Revere house I took a moment to breathe and get my bearings. So, Paul Junior kidnapped me to 1775. I was fine. I would be fine.

Ack! Who was I kidding? I was freaking out! I was in the eighteenth century at the cusp of another war. In the last couple weeks, I'd been to 1929 and alternate versions of my own timeline and now this! Interloping on another traveler's loop could only screw things up further. Getting back to my own timeline now would necessitate catching a ride back to 1929 with Paul Junior, then tripping back to my present—and that's assuming all the loops continue working as before.

The knot in my gut was the size of a boulder and my lungs collapsed against it. Sweat broke out on my brow and I crouched low, bending over slightly to avoid fainting. *Get a grip, Casey*! I was here now, and I had to keep my wits about me if I ever hoped to leave.

"Casey?" Paul Jr. called. "Are you all right?"

"What do you think?" I snapped. "No, I'm not all right. I'm in freaking 1775!"

"I will get you back," he said softly. "I promise, I would not have done this to you had it not been a dire necessity."

My curiosity perked up. I rose carefully, glad to be free of my previous bout of vertigo. "What's going on?"

Paul handed me a burlap bag. "It would be best if you changed first."

I nodded and waited for Paul Junior to give me privacy. "Don't go far," I said. "I'll shout when I'm ready."

Inside the bag was a plain grey dress. I removed my 1920s costume and slipped into the dress. The bodice fit snugly with a wide skirt springing out from my waist, but as usual, the dress was too short, barely touching my ankles. There was no way I was going to get away with wearing this without sticking out, especially with these out-of-era shoes.

"Uh, Paul Junior?"

The bushes rustled and his pale face appeared. He grimaced when he saw my problem.

"I need a needle and thread, a pair of scissors and another dress. An old skirt or under slip would be fine."

As a traveler, Paul Junior would understand the need to be resourceful and quick-thinking. He returned in short order with the required objects, along with a short three-legged stool.

I sat gratefully. "Thanks." I cut the bottom eight inches off the skirt Paul Junior had brought and began the tedious task of sewing it onto the bottom inside seam of my dress. It wouldn't be beautiful, but it should be acceptable enough that people wouldn't stop and stare.

"Now would be a good time to explain," I said as I stitched. "What's so important that you just had to kidnap me?"

Paul Junior's expression was priceless, shocked at the idea that he'd done something illegal.

"Look," I said, softening my voice. "Now's not the time to be shy. Just tell me."

"My sister is secretly seeing a soldier in the Royal Army."

That was the reason? Was he kidding me? "You brought me here to interfere in your sister's love life?"

Paul Junior wiped beads of sweat off his forehead. "No. Yes. You see, I found out what the saying 'One if by land, and two if by sea,' meant. Naturally, I was curious as to why my home had been preserved so far into the future. Why had it not disappeared like most of the Boston I know? When I found out how my father had made history, well, you can imagine my pride.

"I heard him discussing plans to defeat the Regulars…" He glanced away, looking sheepish before continuing. "I listened through the knotholes in the floorboards from the upper level of our house. Later, I came upon Deborah with her ear against the door, also listening."

He pushed dark hair out of his eyes before meeting mine. "I fear she is relaying messages to her soldier."

"That's not very noble, but are you sure it's a problem?" I resumed stitching, otherwise I could be out here all night sewing. "I mean, history has borne itself out already, and your father comes out on top."

His cheeks grew crimson. "Except, I might have said something to arouse her suspicion. I mentioned the code 'One if by land, two if by sea,' before I suspected she might be relaying information to her soldier. I fear I was mistaken that she was on our side when she is not."

The ramifications of what he was saying made me jab the needle into my finger. I winced and popped the wound into my mouth.

Paul Junior continued, "I warned her not to speak a word of it to her soldier, or I would tell father about how she sneaks off to see him, but she would not swear it to me."

Normally, I wouldn't have worried. Whatever happened in the past, has already happened, including any betrayal Deborah might've committed—at least that was how it used to go. Any assurance I used to have about that went out the window with the reset that happened when Adeline and I both tripped at the exact same time while touching each other. Now all the rules had changed.

"Why would she say anything?" I asked. "Does she not hold the same patriot views as your father? Maybe she's curious, but not political enough to act on that information."

"At one time my sister embraced patriotism, but now she is so besotted with this soldier, I would not be surprised if she turned loyalit. Tensions in Boston are high, and folks are very emotional. It's not difficult to feel confused about one's position."

I shifted my skirts so I could reach the back portion. "I still don't get why you need me?"

"Someone has to watch her. Make sure she does not give away father's plan. I do not want her to go down in history for spoiling the early warning system. You of all people understand how important it is that Paul Revere's midnight ride go on without a hitch once the Regulars decide to leave Boston for Lexington and Concord. If Deborah talks, all could be ruined and history altered."

I tied the last knot and stood. Swirling around I checked out the sides and the back. Certainly not runway material but it should do for the here and now.

I didn't know what the heck I was doing anymore, but I did know one thing. That famous midnight ride had to happen. "Okay, I'll help you," I said. "But first, how are you going to explain who I am to your family?"

Clockwork Crazy

Chapter Eleven

Your family left Boston when the British arrived. Many patriots have done this, so it will not be hard to believe," Paul Junior said. "You remained to care for an aunt, a loyalist who was too frail and stubborn to leave with the family. She died recently and the loyalists commandeered her house and you are left with nowhere to go."

I cocked a brow. "I see you thought this through?"

Paul Junior's expression remained solemn. "I've lain awake many nights."

"What's my aunt's name and where's my house?"

He cut me a look. "There is no aunt in actuality."

"I know that. But you have to be prepared for questions. Believe me, people will ask, and we have to get our story straight."

"Very well, the house is in Southend. We rarely leave Boston proper, so no one will assume to know the street. You pick a name."

"Eloise Donovan." My mother's name and easy to remember. "How did we meet?"

Paul Junior scratched the patchy scruff on his chin. "You were crying in the square, homeless."

Acting confused and somewhat distraught wasn't a stretch from how I was actually feeling. "Fine. Let's go inside and you can make introductions."

I picked up my skirts as we crossed the Revere courtyard. It wasn't anything like the museum version. This once had chickens running about freely, a milk cow tethered to a pole, and a good-sized vegetable garden. A couple little girls ran over to Paul Junior as we walked by and grabbed his pant legs. He rubbed their dark heads.

"These are my little sisters Sarah and Mary," he said with a smile. "Girls, this is my friend Miss Donovan."

I said hello and offered my hand. They suddenly became very timid and drew back behind Paul Junior. "They are shy," he said, "but do not worry. After a few days, they will be your shadows and you will not be able to shake them off."

We walked into the kitchen, which smelled of fresh bread and warm milk. The flooring of wide wooden planks had dirt in the cracks and unwashed dishes remained on a long, wooden table with more piled in a wash bin— evidence that the place was lived in, a contrast to the tidy, spotless, roped-off museum version I knew.

The walls and ceilings were a mix of dark wood and bright white stucco. Copper and cast-iron pots and pans hung from one of the wooden beams. A multi-coloured brick fireplace took up most of one wall.

A baby wearing a thick wad of cloth diapers was strapped into a wooden high chair and a petite, tired-looking woman spooned food into its mouth. I assumed she was Rachel Walker, Paul Revere's second wife.

"Stepmother," Paul Junior said, confirming my guess. The woman turned at his voice, but her eyes landed on me. "This is Miss Casey Donovan, and she is in need of housing for a short while. Her aunt died and the loyalists took the house."

Rachel stood and offered a smile. "Of course, you may stay." She extended a hand. "I'm Mrs. Revere. I'm sorry for your loss."

"Thank you," I said. "I will help out as much as I can. I'd be happy to do the dishes." I took in the plump toddler behind her. I'd rather do dishes than change diapers.

"Of course, any help would be appreciated." At that moment, Sarah and Mary ran through the room, shouting and hooting. Rachel's smile fell. "The children can be a handful."

A male voice floated our way. "We must entreat the other colonists to join us. Pennsylvania, Virginia..."

Two men entered the room and their conversation ceased when they saw us.

"Good morning," the shorter of the two men said to me. With his square face and dark eyes, he resembled

Paul Junior, and also, in a weird way, Jack Black, and I knew immediately who he was. Paul Revere, *in the flesh!*

"Pa," Paul Junior began. "This is Casey Donovan." He repeated the tale we'd concocted about a fictitious, dead aunt. "Stepmother said she could stay for a while."

"Of course," Paul Revere said. He reached for my hand. "We're happy to assist you in any way."

I stretched out my hand and allowed Paul Revere to encase it with his large, rough palm. I had a hard time keeping my jaw from dropping as my mind tried to register this surreal moment. This was *Paul Revere!* The famous midnight rider. A patriarch of our nation. I felt a little light-headed.

I managed to respond with a fluttering of lashes and a stupid grin. Paul Revere motioned to his friend, a slender man, with a ponytail similar to the loose one at the nape of Paul Revere's neck. He wore a long coat over top of a cotton shirt, and dungarees tucked into tall, leather boots. "This is Samuel Adams."

Oh my gosh! I really did feel weak in the knees. Paul Junior pushed a chair toward me. "Maybe you should sit down."

"I'm sorry," I said weakly. "I'm not usually…"

"You look a little pale Miss Donovan," Samuel Adams said. "Should I call for Dr. Warren?"

I shook my head. I didn't think I could handle an encounter with another famous patriot just yet. "I'm fine," I said. "Just a lot has happened recently."

"Perhaps you'd like to lie down?" Rachel asked.

"Or, a little fresh air?" The question was a suggestion, but I could see by the widening of Paul Junior's dark eyes that he wanted to leave.

"Yes, a little air would be good. Would you mind accompanying me, Paul Junior?"

Paul Junior nodded and stepped forward to give me his arm.

"It really was a pleasure to meet you all," I blurted out. Paul Junior picked up the pace, almost dragging me out into the courtyard.

"I'm sorry," I said, looking over my shoulder. "I've never met anyone so famous before. Not in any timeline I've visited. Not even in my own. I confess to being a little star struck."

"Please do get your sensibility under control, Casey. It is imperative that no one suspect you."

"Suspect me of what? Impersonating a person from the future?"

"No. Of being a spy."

"But I'm not a spy!"

"Well, I know that... but everyone in Boston is very anxious right now." He stiffened. "Oh, here comes Deborah."

Deborah was a pretty girl, with hazel eyes, dark tendrils of hair spilling out from under a gray bonnet, and an emerald green cape over a dark full-skirted dress. She slowed momentarily when she saw us, then attempted a casual manner that seemed forced. Her rosy cheeks and the flush on her neck spoke of a recent illicit encounter.

"Deborah!" Paul Junior called her over and began introductions, reciting once again my story about the dead aunt and lost house. Deborah murmured her condolences. "Stepmother insisted that she stay with us, since she has nowhere to go."

Deborah's lips tightened at the mention of Rachel and I wondered if there were some tensions there. It wouldn't be surprising. No one liked to feel that their mother could be so easily replaced. But Paul Revere had had many children with his first wife, and I could see why he had wanted to marry again quickly, just to have help around the house. Rachel was to be commended for taking it on, in my opinion.

"I suppose she'll have to share my chamber," Deborah said.

Deborah also wasn't thrilled to have me around, if I could go by how she was referring to me in third person in my presence.

"Yes," Paul Junior said. "Please show her your hospitality and your kindness."

Deborah peeled off a pair of gloves, an accessory that seemed incongruent with the rest of her wardrobe. I wondered if they were a gift from the British soldier. "Of course." She looked me in the eyes then. "Please come with me."

I followed Deborah up a narrow set of stairs to the second floor and to a bedroom overlooking the street. It was small but neat with a double bed on a wooden frame and a hand-quilted blanket spread tidily over top. The walls were bright white, meeting more stained wood halfway down from the ceiling. I lowered myself into a chair, which stood by the wooden desk that was pressed up against one of the walls

Deborah stared at me like she wasn't quite sure what to do with me. "I'm truly sorry to hear about your loss."

"Thank you. It means so much to me." I thought I'd throw a bit more drama in, just to see her response. "It was awful losing my aunt, but I could've managed alone on my own for awhile, at least until someone from my family in the colonies could come for me. But the regulars just tossed me out on the street, with no compassion at all."

Deborah grew still. "They, unfortunately, were only following orders."

"Do you think they're justified in taking property that doesn't belong to them?"

"It is only because of the rebellion. Loyalists have no need to worry about mistreatment. I do not mean to sound unkind, but the King requires certain…behaviours and duties… from his subjects."

"My aunt and I are no threat to the British army or His Royal Highness."

She eyed me pointedly. "So you say."

"I do say."

"Of course. I meant no insult." Deborah removed her cap and cape and hung them on hooks behind her door. "I admit, some members of the King's army can be…harsh. But they are not all like that."

"Oh?" I sat up with my hands resting on my lap, and an eager look on my face. I assumed girls in the eighteenth century were just as keen to talk about their crushes as girls in the twenty-first century were.

"Tell me something, Casey. Have you ever loved a man?"

"Yes," I responded quickly. "But, he's beyond my reach." I hoped my confession would make Deborah feel like she could relate to me.

She tilted her head and watched me. "Do you still love him?"

I nodded. "Yes."

"Why is he beyond your reach?"

I didn't know how to answer this. I didn't want her thinking that I too, had my eyes on a British soldier.

Deborah answered for me. "Do your parents think he is a bad match?"

"Um…" I shrugged. "They think he's too old for me."

Deborah wrinkled her nose. "Men are never the ones that are too old. There must be another opposition. Does he belong to another?"

I thought about the timeline where he was with Lucinda and the last one where he was with Jessica. "You could say that." I decided to elaborate. "It's why I agreed to stay with my aunt. It was just too painful to remain in Boston."

"And now your heartache continues."

"What about you?" I asked turning the tables. "Is there someone special in your life?"

I'd hoped that with me sharing my love story/fable, she would do the same. Her eyes sparkled and it was obvious that she was thinking of someone. Her lips parted and I readied myself for her tale, but then her mouth closed. She busied herself with tidying up, avoiding my eyes.

"I really should let you rest. Shall I call you for dinner?"

My stomach had been complaining for some time now. "That would be nice."

"Fine. I will see to it that you are summoned."

Deborah Revere disappeared and I let out a sigh. I didn't know what Paul Junior thought I would accomplish, but I felt like I'd just failed the first test.

Exhaustion was my friend and it took nanoseconds for me to drift asleep after crawling into Deborah's bed. Eventually my dream world morphed as I slipped back to consciousness with its hard realities and it took me some moments to register where I was and why. I suppressed a low moan and let myself stay in the loose state of slumber, unwilling to end the comfort found on this feather bed.

The door creaked open, and I half expected a tap announcing dinner. I opened my eyes just enough to see Deborah ease in with a candle in one hand. She moved about stealthily and I thought I'd pretend to sleep a little longer, just to see if she'd do something worth reporting back to Paul Junior. Her figure cast large shadows across the darkened room and I wondered for the first time what time it was and if maybe I'd slept through supper.

Deborah opened a dresser drawer, withdrew a piece of paper and slipped it into the bodice of her dress. Her gaze moved over me and I played dead. Deborah tiptoed out the door and slowly closed it.

I jumped out of bed.

Elle Strauss

Chapter Twelve

Deborah floated down the steps and I worried I'd lose sight of her before we even left the house. The natural creaking of the floorboards and the wooden stairwell were swallowed by the chatter of young voices and the clattering of dishes coming from the kitchen.

I pressed myself against the shadows in the darkening living area, until Deborah disappeared through the front door. I hurried after her, plucking a dark cape off a hook and exiting onto the street, which was surprisingly close to the house. Pedestrians meandered by, a sea of brown linen dresses, dirty-white shirts and drab cloaks.

I made sure to keep enough distance and ducked on more than one occasion when she took a furtive glance over her shoulder. Despite keeping my eyes locked on the back of her head, I couldn't miss how vastly different this

Boston was from my own—almost all wooden structures, with only prominent buildings like churches and halls made out of the red brick that is so iconic in the Boston of my own day.

This Boston was wretched. Muddy, soiled streets, bad smells, and unhappy, impoverished citizens. Amongst the plainly dressed where a number of redcoats. The red-tail coats, trimmed elegantly with gold-colored buttons, worn over white pants, shirt and vest were such a contrast. The resentment held by many of the colonists was etched on their faces and more than one dirty-faced man spit in the street when a soldier of the Royal Army passed by.

I held a sleeve over my nose to stave off the odor, a posture that also helped to hide my face, should Deborah glance behind her.

Boston harbor came into view and I stopped short, stunned by what I saw. A multitude of large battleships bristling with tall masts holding up massive sails floated in the harbor. Holes along the wooden hulls spoke of the damage they were capable of when their canons were set loose. They were majestic and awe-inspiring, demanding respect—and getting it from me.

I'd stared open-mouthed for too long. Oh no—Deborah! I scanned the crowds, rushing to the cross roads and peering down alleys. I let out a frustrated groan. I'd lost her!

Some help I was. Good thing Paul Junior had gone to the trouble to drag me back in time to right history and our future. Good thing!

Elle Strauss

I continued my search heading into Quincy Market, which was only a single smaller building and once again covered my face to ward off the strong fish stench coming from the open stalls. Many of the vendors were busy closing up shop as the last of the evening sunlight melted away.

I circled back, thinking Deborah might've taken a circuitous route in case she was being followed (by me!). I was almost ready to admit defeat and begin the search for the Revere house when I caught sight of her distinctive green cape as she entered the Old North Church. I quickly approached the iconic red-brick building with its white tower poking the darkening sky.

I opened the church door super-slowly to avoid any complaint from the hinges and slipped inside. Deborah was obviously meeting someone here. Her British soldier? It seemed like an odd place to have a romantic rendezvous. My stomach folded over at the thought that Paul Revere's daughter would repeat patriot strategy to the opposition, words she overheard in her own house.

I already knew from my own visits to the Old North Church that it didn't contain rows of pews like most churches, but instead had pew cubicles, almost like in twenty-first century office buildings. The four walls that surrounded each box were tall enough to hide the identity of the occupants. On a Sunday, the preacher climbed steps to a raised podium in order to be seen and heard by the parishioners.

Deborah had disappeared into one of the cubicles but I didn't know which one. Holding the rail with one hand and hiking my skirt up with the other, I raced up the steps to the balcony. From there I could see the top of Deborah's head, brown curls cascading down her back from under her bonnet. I automatically touched my bare head, only now realizing that it was probably the reason for the many stares I had gotten along the way.

She sat on a bench beside a man wearing the unmistakable red of the British uniform. He had his hands on her cheeks and they stared at each other longingly, eye to eye. My hand went to my chest as I held my breath, feeling like a sleazy Peeping Tom when they leaned in for the kiss.

My heart squeezed tight. I remembered the day when Nate and I exchanged such passionate encounters, and we didn't have anyone telling us we couldn't be together. How awful to fall for someone whose ideals run opposite to those of your family. To have your love forbidden by those who are close to you.

And like Nate and me, if for differing reasons, poor Deborah Revere was bound for heartache! There was no way this relationship would last. At least, if I could assume that history would go unchanged. By this time next year, the British regiment would be preparing to leave Boston, and Deborah would go on to meet a nice Patriot man and have lots of American children.

I concealed myself behind a supporting beam, peeking out just enough to watch the drama beneath me unfold. Their whispering floated upward but I could only pick out partial sentences.

"...I wish we could be together always..."

"...When the rebellion is quashed..."

Before I knew it, Deborah removed the folded sheet of paper from the bodice of her dress. The soldier accepted it and opened it swiftly.

Oh no! I'd failed to stop the transfer of intel! I could call out, but what would that do? The soldier already had the information.

"You're sure?" he asked.

Deborah nodded. He kissed her again, then left her alone in the pew. I pulled back out of his line of vision until I heard the door click shut.

Tears flowed down Deborah's cheeks as she sat there sobbing quietly, alone.

Oh, Deborah. What have you done?

I snuck out of the church before she left and meandered through the narrow, crooked streets. Nothing was recognizable to me and I experienced a moment of panic, feeling utterly lost until I suddenly happened upon the Revere House. Then I searched for Paul Junior.

I found Rachel scrubbing dishes in the kitchen.

"I'm so sorry," I said on seeing her. She looked worn out, with stiff shoulders and dark circles under her eyes. "I said I would help you, and I've slept the afternoon away."

Her eyes flashed with something like envy, and I had the feeling she'd give her right arm to have a whole afternoon to sleep.

"Let me finish those for you."

"If you are willing, I'll not decline." Rachel let out a long sigh. "Normally I depend on Deborah's help. But lately…"

"It's fine," I said. "I don't mind."

I thrust my hands into murky, tepid water and began scrubbing. "Have you seen Paul Junior?" I asked. "I'd like to thank him again for bringing me here."

"He's in the shop working with his father. They often work late into the night."

I suspected much of the work these days took the form of strategizing. I wish I had heard more of the conversation between Deborah and her soldier. I didn't really have any news to offer Paul Junior other than to confirm that a conversation (and a kissing session!) took place. I didn't know for certain what was on the sheet of paper. It could be the lantern code.

"Is the shop nearby?" I asked.

Rachel paused and sent me a strange look. "Aye, but women are not allowed inside. You best wait here for him." She set a loaf of bread on the table. "I expect that it has been a while since you've eaten."

My stomach growled in response. She pointed to the kettle on the hearth. "There is some broth left in the pot. I hope you don't mind if I take my leave?"

"Of course. You've been more than generous."

105

Rachel left me alone and I decided to leave the dishes until after I had eaten. I was famished! I cut a thick slice of bread and used a ladle to fill up a porcelain bowl with a thin soup.

The broth wasn't exactly hot and the bread was on the dry side, but I didn't care. I dipped it into the broth and practically inhaled it.

When I finished, I put the rest of the bread back in the bin Rachel had retrieved it from and went back to scrubbing the pots.

I stoked the fire, adding another log. It not only provided heat, but light, the room had grown gloomy with the setting of the sun.

The back door swung open and Paul Junior rushed into the kitchen, eyes wild.

"It's happening!"

I stared back at him. "What's happening?"

"The Regulars are moving out!"

I dried my hands, wishing I had my smartphone. "What date is it?"

"It is the Year of Our Lord 1775, the eighteenth of April."

I knew it was close to the date of the midnight ride, but I'd lost track of time with all the tripping back and forth.

"Dr. Warren received word somehow," Paul Junior said. "Except he doesn't know if it is by land or by sea."

"It's by sea."

"Are you sure?"

"I... well, that's what happened before. But I supposed things might've changed," I said. "Deborah might know."

Paul Junior blinked. "Deborah? How?"

"She slipped out while the rest of you were eating. I followed her to the Old North Church..."

Confusion spread across his face. "The Old North Church?"

Right. I supposed it wasn't considered old yet.

Paul Junior clarified. "You mean Christ Church?"

"Yes. Deborah met with her soldier there. She gave him a note." I decided it wouldn't do any good to bring up the kissing session.

"We have to find her."

Suddenly Deborah stood before us. "Find who?"

"Sister, you!" Paul Junior grabbed her arm and stared hard into her eyes. "What did you tell your Regular at Christ Church? What was in the note? We must know!"

Deborah flinched and I didn't know if it was because of the grip Paul Junior had on her arm, or the fact that she had been found out.

"Let go of me."

Paul Junior inhaled and huffed as he released his hold. "Have you betrayed our father?"

"Have you betrayed our king?"

"He's no king of mine."

"Mine neither."

"What?"

Deborah hadn't cried herself out earlier, since the water works turned on again full force. I handed her a tea-towel and she collapsed onto a chair.

"I lied to Clive. I love him, but I lied, and he'll know I lied." She sobbed into the towel. "I know I will never see him again."

Paul Junior knelt at her feet, his voice softening. "What did you tell him, Deborah?"

She stared at him with an expression of regret and grief. "I told him the militiamen were stockpiling arms in Charleston."

"Instead of Concord?" I asked.

She nodded my way with a perplexed look. "How do you know about Concord?"

I shrugged. Paul Junior deflected by adding, "Father is preparing to cross the river to Cambridge to warn the militiamen of the army's plans to leave Boston." He stood. "I must assist him at the boat house."

"I'll go with you."

"No, Casey. This is a man's job."

"I'm going to pretend you didn't just say that." I helped myself to the cape I'd worn early and draped it over my shoulders. Then I followed Paul Junior into the night.

I thought about Deborah with deep sadness. She obviously loved this soldier, but betrayed him anyway. She put her love for her colony and her family before her heart. I imagined having to make such a choice, choosing between Nate and the greater good (assuming he hadn't already ended it with me). It was one thing to be left. Another to do the leaving when you really didn't want to go.

Paul Junior knew his way in the dark. I hurried to keep up, since I didn't know the layout of this Boston at all, and the lack of streetlights made it even more difficult.

I heard the rippling of the Charles River before I saw it. The softening of the soil beneath my feet was another indicator we'd drawn close. It was odd to look across with only the light of a partial moon and not see brilliant city lights from Cambridge. Instead there was a spattering of lantern lights on a nearby British man-of-war vessel I could only assume was the *Somerset*.

Paul Revere waited by a wooden shed. He cocked a brow when he saw me with Paul Junior, but decided against questioning it.

"Son, I need your assistance in carrying the canoe. Miss Donovan, perhaps you can carry the oars?"

I gathered up the wooden oars in question, noting that they had been padded with old cloth, presumably to prevent the slapping sound in the water.

Paul Junior hoisted one end of the canoe up onto his shoulder with a grunt.

"We must refrain from speaking from this point onward," Paul Revere said.

I followed them as we continued to the riverside in silence. From my peripheral vision I spotted two lights twinkling high over the darkness of the city. I smiled. Lanterns in the Old North Church.

109

I wondered how effective Deborah's fib would be. Would the army head to Charleston first? Their diversion would definitely buy the militiamen some time.

Or they would spread their resources out, and thus minimizing the effect. Perhaps Deborah betrayed her love for no reason.

Paul Revere seemed a little unsteady to me as we pushed him off in the canoe. He paddled away from shore while Paul Junior and I nervously watched.

The small vessel lilted. Something was wrong!

Paul Revere whispered loudly, "There's a leak!"

What? This wasn't how it was supposed to go!

Paul Junior ran into the water. "He can't swim!"

I tore off my cape and jumped in, gasping as the cold water soaked through my skirt. Together Paul Junior and I grabbed onto the canoe and pushed it to shore, where Paul Revere toppled out. At least the water wasn't over his head and the current was mild. We shook ourselves off like wet dogs. I couldn't even grasp what just happened.

"You there!" Two British soldiers appeared out of the darkness, rifles at the ready.

I felt dizzy and fell, totally missing out on whatever happened next.

Chapter Thirteen

My brain wasn t running on all four cylinders. I'd tripped from 1775, and once again wore my flapper-style dress, but the cars and noise around me were definitely the twenty-first century.

I seriously felt like I was going crazy. Everything was so screwed up!

My synapses misfired and I stepped out into the streets like I was doped. Horns blasted and people shouted obscenities. Someone pulled me back onto the sidewalk.

"Are you okay, miss?" The man had an accent, Australian or British maybe. He wore a sharp business suit and studied me through wire-rimmed glasses.

"I'm fine," I mumbled. "Just lost."

Satisfied with that response, he hurried across the intersection. So long as I wasn't dead or bleeding, he didn't need to bother with a stranger like me. At least he'd taken the time to pull me off the busy street. I wouldn't have wanted to inconvenience him with an accident or a police inquiry.

Most of the pedestrians, dressed in somber blues or blacks, walked quickly to some urgent destination. Many had their heads bent down looking at the smartphones in their hands, or strolled with hands in front pockets while they listened to music or podcasts only they could hear through their ear buds.

It was a relief to be back, though I didn't understand how it happened. The time travel laws had been broken, it seemed irrevocably, and I might never again know what to expect.

The thought made my heart palpitate.

I straightened my shoulders and smoothed out my frock. I was in the north end of Boston and needed to get back to Cambridge. I didn't have any money for the train or a phone to make a call.

Who would I call if I could? Not Nate. Lucinda or Tim? But how? Did Boston even have any pay phones anymore?

Even if there were some, I didn't have a debit card or a single coin.

I must've looked quite deranged. I jumped at a tapping on my shoulder.

"I'm sorry, miss, didn't mean to frighten you."

I stared into the eyes of a female African-American police officer. Coincidentally, she also had an accent. "I'm officer Givens," she said. "Do you need assistance?"

She was probably thinking medical assistance, like psych ward!

"I need a ride home," I admitted. "I don't have any money."

"Is there someone you can call?" Officer Givens produced a cell phone. She cocked a brow "A parent, maybe?"

No doubt she not only wondered why I was dressed this way, but also why I wasn't in school. And, now that she mentioned it, getting picked up by my mother sounded like a good option. I wouldn't even mind being fussed over right now. I would love for someone else to be in charge of my life for a while.

I recited my mom's cell number and prayed it was correct. It started ringing and Officer Givens handed me the phone.

"Hi, Mom. I'm in Boston and I need to be picked up."

"What on earth are you doing in Boston?" Mom's phone carried, and I could tell by the officer's smirk, that she could hear her, too. I wondered if the officer had a kid at home that caused her trouble.

"It's hard to explain. I don't have my purse..."

"Were you mugged?"

Officer Givens shot me a look. I subtly shook my head.

"No, mom. I just... forgot it. Please, I have no way to get home and I need a ride."

"Oh Casey, I'm right in the middle of a very important contract, but Nate's here looking for you. He says he'll come."

My blood swooshed at the mention of his name. "Nate's looking for me?"

She either didn't hear my question or ignored it. "Where are you exactly?"

I recited the address and promised her I'd wait. "Please be careful!"

"I will, Mom."

"I'm on foot patrol," Officer Givens said as she slid her phone away. "I'll wait with you until your ride comes. Tell me your name."

"Casey Donovan, and I'm fine, really," I said, feeling like a bother now.

"It's okay, Miss Donovan, I don't mind waiting."

Passersby gawked briefly at me with the officer, but averted their eyes and continued on. I wondered what they all found so interesting and then I caught my reflection in the shop mirror.

Horror! My hair was a fly-away, knotted mess and looked like it hadn't been washed in days, (which it hadn't). My dress was torn and askew and I wore the boots Paul Junior had given me to wear while hiding out by the river. They were damp with mud.

Oh, man. How was I going to explain this to Nate?

I motioned to the officer. "Hey, would you happen to have a brush? Or comb?"

Her eyes flashed with disbelief. "Sorry, Miss. Not a beauty-supply shop."

Elle Strauss

I started to sweat at the thought of my imminent encounter with Nate, and surreptitiously sniffed at my armpits. Not too bad. I smelled a little like swamp.

While waiting on a Boston city street corner with a police officer was awkward, the anticipation of seeing Nate again was the source of real anxiety. Suddenly his old BMW turned the corner and pulled up to a stop in front of me. His dark hair was tousled just the way I liked it, his jaw covered faintly in bristles. His stunning blue eyes were wide with wonder—or was it shock? His mouth dropped open as he studied me.

Officer Givens bent over to speak into the opened window. "Your name?"

"Nate Mackenzie."

She looked at me. "You're comfortable with getting into the car with this man?"

I nodded my head.

"Mr. Mackenzie, take her straight home to her mother. I've noted your license plate number. I will be calling in one hour to make sure she's delivered safely."

"Yes, ma'am," he said.

I pulled on my earlobe. Why did everyone sound like they had a foreign accent?

I let myself in the passenger side and buckled up. I remembered to poke my head out the window to say thanks to Officer Givens in time before we disappeared into traffic.

Nate openly gawked at me, his eyes back and forth to the road ahead. "What's going on with you?"

"Hi," I returned. "Why were you with my mom?"

116

"Looking for you. What happened? Casey? No offense, but you look terrible."

"I tripped." I pulled down the visor, looked at my reflection and inwardly moaned.

"You fell down?"

My gaze cut to Nate. "I tripped."

"You said that. But that doesn't explain why you're in Boston and dressed like that."

My heart sank. He didn't know what I meant by "tripped." This wasn't *my* Nate. This wasn't *my* timeline. Again.

I let my head drop back and closed my eyes. What "new" reality was I to encounter now?

I felt Nate's hand on mine and my eyes flicked open.

"I know I've been gone a while," he said. Nate slowed as he pulled into at strip mall parking lot, stopping in a stall. He turned to face me. "I should've called. Australia's on the other side of the world, but if I'd known…"

"Wait, what? Australia?" What happened to Spain? "Is that why you're talking like that? You've picked up an accent."

"Maybe. I just got back last night. But, you're the one talking funny."

What did he mean by that?

He placed a hand on the back of my neck and pulled me close. "I missed you."

Oh, how I missed his touch and the look of tenderness in his eyes. He wrapped me in a hug and I almost started bawling.

"This might sound like a strange question," I said weakly, "but, are we together?"

Nate pulled back and locked his baby blues on mine. "Of course we are."

Then he kissed me.

And I kissed him back.

This might not be my Nate, but in that moment, I didn't care. I threw myself into his kiss even though I looked like an overgrown, brunette version of little orphan Annie. I was tired and emotionally distraught, worn out and exhausted. I just wanted to be with Nate and here he was!

"Whoa," Nate said with a chuckle. "I have to get you home before Officer Givens has me arrested."

He pulled back out onto the Mass Pike and I sighed. Nate and Casey were together. For this moment in time, it was all I cared about.

He turned on some music and I was happy to listen to anything that wasn't ragtime or jazz.

"Tell me about Australia," I said. I hoped if I kept him talking, I'd get some clue as to what I'd be facing.

"It's hot. Surfing's great."

He half grinned at me. "Was a mistake to go without you."

"I'm sorry."

"Why? It wasn't your fault. The guys said no girlfriends, otherwise I'd have brought you along." He patted my thigh. "Next time."

Next time? He really didn't know about my no-long-flights-across-large-bodies-of-water rule.

"Who did you go with?" I asked.

"Did you bump your head when you fell?"

I opted to say nothing, hoping he'd just keep talking. It worked.

"Chuck and Stan, my roomies at York, remember?"

York! This Nate didn't go to BU! He went to college in Toronto when he wasn't gallivanting around the globe with "the guys."

"Don't worry," Nate continued. "I'm home for the summer." Another crooked grin. "I'm all yours."

This should make me happy. Nate Mackenzie just vowed to be mine for the next two to three months. If his term had ended with time for him to go to Australia that meant it wasn't April anymore. I wondered at the warm weather. Did that mean I'd already graduated in this timeline?

Nate's phone lay face up between us. It glowed with the date and time. June 2nd, 2:15 pm.

I not only jumped from another traveler's loop to an alternate version of my own, I lost several weeks. I couldn't keep up. The whole thing was making me crazy.

We entered Cambridge and I found I just wanted to go home and to bed. I was so exhausted.

119

Nate was done talking and now he wanted me to have a turn. "I know you fell and hit your head, but what were you doing out of school, and why are you dressed like that?"

I bit the inside of my lip. "Well, you're never going to believe it."

He waited for me to continue and I inhaled, wondering what kind of story was about to come out of my mouth.

"I haven't been sleeping well. Like at all. I think I have a sleeping disorder."

"Okay. But how did that get you in Boston looking like that?"

"Maybe I'm also sleepwalking. Lucid dreaming. I might've caught the Red Line while being completely unaware. In fact, I do have a foggy memory of doing so. I've caught that line into Boston so many times, I could've quite literally done it in my sleep."

"Casey, that's scary."

The scary part was how quickly I came up with that lie. It was a doozy. I finished it off with, "I really don't know how I got there."

"Well, you're home and safe now."

I sighed at his thoughtful concern. Then I frowned. Nate pulled into the driveway of a unit in a row of town homes.

I live here? Not my house? Not even the apartment building my mother and I once lived in. I didn't see Mom's car in the drive or parked on the street.

"I thought she was home?" I said.

"No, she's at work."

"But you were with her?"

"I was looking for you."

"Why would I be there?"

His brow furrowed over worried eyes. "Uh, because you work there? Did you quit without telling me?"

"No, I …"

Nate cupped the back of my head with his hand and stared into my eyes with deep concern. "I'm worried about you. Please promise you'll see a doctor?"

I couldn't promise that but I told him what he wanted to hear. "Okay."

He leaned in and touched his forehead to mine. I inhale his musky scent and reached for his neck.

"I missed you so much," I whispered. I pinched back the tears that threatened. I just wished he remembered me—the traveler me. I felt so alone, like the burden of this mixed up world rested solely on my shoulders.

"I missed you, too." He said. He tilted his face so his lips could connect with mine. He wasn't my Nate and I wasn't his Casey, and it was probably wrong of me to kiss him. But I still didn't care.

Chapter Fourteen

It took every ounce of willpower to pull myself away from Nate's warm embrace, but if I didn't go in, I was in danger of falling asleep in his arms to the white noise of his idling car engine.

I stepped outside and froze. A flag hung from a pole in the centre of the cul-de-sac and it wasn't the stars and stripes. It had a distinctive red-on-white cross over x on a royal blue background. The Union Jack fluttered in the breeze.

I stammered, "We're B-british?"

"Casey, are you all right?"

I bent low to stare at Nate through the passenger window. "We're *British*?"

"Yes," he said slowly. "Always have been. What exactly is going on?"

I stood and groaned. The midnight ride never happened. The militiamen hadn't been warned! No Declaration of Independence! No July 4th holiday!

Nate waited for me to enter my house, but I had one minor problem. The door was locked and I didn't have a key. I glanced back awkwardly. I couldn't even get into my own home.

Nate waved me over.

"There's a spare under the garden gnome."

"Right." I said. There was a narrow flower bed underneath what I imagined was the living room window. A little red-hatted gnome was tucked under a particularly thorny rose bush. I tilted the little man and stole the key he was protecting, but not without snagging the skin on the top of my hand.

"Ow!"

"You all right?" Nate called.

"Yeah, just got caught on a thorn." I hurried to the front door so that Nate wouldn't have to wait there all night. I wiped the dirty key on my dress and slipped it into the lock, feeling relieved when the door swung open.

"I'll ring you later," Nate said before he backed out. All sorts of mixed emotions swirled through me as I waved.

The blinds were drawn and the rooms before me were drearily dark. I switched on a lamp. If Mom was still in interior design, it was hard to tell by this place. It was clean, and cozy in a shabby chic way, but nothing like the modern flair of hers that I was used to.

The kitchen was small but tidy, and if I hadn't been so tired, I might've searched the cupboards for food. Apprehension prickled my skin as I looked around. I hadn't seen any signs of masculinity. No large-sized shoes at the door, no coats or hoodies that might belong to Tim and my dad.

I sighed as I climbed the steps to where I assumed the bedrooms were. Here was another reality where my parents didn't make it. It seemed the odds were against them, and it made me even more thankful that they actually were able to work things out in my own time. I would never take that for granted again. I just hoped I got back there eventually.

I found my mom's room, which had its own bathroom. Nice, that meant I didn't have to share the one in the hall. My room was similar in style to all of the other bedrooms I'd occupied in the various realms. I was becoming predictable.

I decided on a quick shower, crawled into bed, and then fell into a coma.

My eyes fluttered as I came to a slow, fuzzy awareness of my Mother's face hovering over me.

"Honey," she said. "Why are you sleeping in the middle of the day?"

It was weird to hear her speak with an accent. Her blond hair was longer than I had ever seen it before and pulled into a messy bun on the top of her head. She wore dress pants and a silk blouse, like she was dressed to go out.

"Are you going somewhere?" I asked, adding a faux lilt to my voice. I didn't want to give her reason to think things were more off than they were already.

"No, silly," she said. "I just got home from work. What happened to you today?"

I wanted to ask her where she worked but that would make her even more concerned about me. I'd have to get my information about this world another way later on.

"I caught a ride into Boston after school with my friends," I answered, "and we got separated." It was a lame excuse. At least I didn't have to explain my previous disheveled appearance or the costume.

Mom squinted. "Why didn't you call them? That's why I bought you a phone."

"I forgot it at home." I could see a brown leather saddlebag purse sitting on the floor by my closet. "I grabbed my backpack, but totally forgot to take my purse."

Mom stroked my forehead, moving curls off my face. "You need to be more careful," she said softly. "I couldn't stand to lose you."

I blinked at what sounded a teensy bit melodramatic. "Well, now Nate's home," she continued, "so I can rest easier. He'll take care of you."

She *wanted* Nate to take care of me? This wasn't the same woman who thought I was too young to be getting so serious with Nate back when I was planning my fateful trip to Hollywood. Man, that felt like an eternity ago.

Mom stifled a yawn. "I'm knackered, too. Go back to sleep and I'll see you in the morning."

Getting back to sleep wasn't so easy. I tossed and turned and fluffed my pillow, but my mind wouldn't rest. I decided to call Lucinda, find a way to get her to brief me on what was going on in this timeline without, hopefully, sounding like a crazy person.

Besides, I had no idea how I was getting to school in the morning. I was going to be so glad when graduation was over so I didn't have to keep learning to navigate a new high school ecosystem every time I tripped.

I gathered my purse off the floor and fished out my phone. For some reason Lucinda's name wasn't on speed dial, but I knew her number by heart and tapped it in.

"Hey, Lucinda," I said when she answered. "It's Casey."

"Stop calling me!"

I froze to the spot, stunned by her harsh words. "What?"

"You guys need to leave me alone!"

"What?" I repeated. "Wait. What's going on?"

"I gave you what you wanted, now sod off." She hung up and I worked to pick my jaw up off the floor.

Not only were Lucinda and I not friends, we were hostile? I couldn't imagine a scenario where that could be true. Lucinda and I had been best friends forever. I never would've survived middle school if it weren't for her.

So if Lucinda wasn't my friend, then who was? I assumed I had friends. I searched my phone for clues and swallowed thickly as I stared at the name on the top of my speed dial list. Jessica Fuller. I scrolled through the text messages and sure enough, most of them were a conversation between her and me.

Life was just too crazy!

I awoke to my alarm the next morning feeling like I'd been out on a drunken spree, or pulled along the highway by a truck. Not that I'd ever done either, but I could only imagine. Thankfully, Mom had a pot of coffee on. I still didn't know who was taking me to school. It wasn't Tim or Lucinda, obviously, so maybe Jessica? Or Mom? I figured I'd just wait until it was time to go and get into whatever vehicle arrived.

The me in this timeline had nice clothes, and it felt good to get back into a pair of comfortable jeans. I didn't want to deal with my hair, so I wore it back in a low pony. I chose a soft long-sleeved blouse, and finished off my look with a cotton spring coat and black ballet slip-ons.

I hoped I'd already done my homework, if I had any. I used to want to graduate with honors and now I would just be happy to graduate—preferable in my own timeline!

I watched out the living room window, wondering if maybe Nate was the one to pick me up. But, no, he'd just gotten back to town. It must be someone else.

Mom slipped into her jacket and shoes and draped the strap of her purse over her shoulder. So, Mom was my chauffeur.

Then she waved and said, "See you tonight," adding as an afterthought, "Shouldn't you get going? You're going to miss your bus."

Ugh! I took the bus? I had no idea about the routes to Cambridge High from here.

"Yeah, I'll leave in a minute," I said. She drove off and I pulled up the website for transit routes and times. There was a stop at the end of the street. A bus would arrive in five minutes that would take me to a stop a block from the school. I locked up the house, remembering to put the spare house key back under the gnome and headed down the road.

The townhouse complex was a mass of bright red bricks with black trim. Though it was a common enough look for these parts I couldn't help feeling a sense of déjà vu.

I knew why. It was because I'd been here before, many times. This was the same complex Uncle Samuel lived in! Only in my timeline, these were occupied by people fifty-five years of age or older. I searched for #24 and saw a brown face with crows feet around the eyes and graying hair watching me from the window. He smiled and raised a hand in a wave.

I raised a hand back. I wanted to stop in and tell him all about my misadventures, not caring that I would miss my bus and a day of school.

But, maybe he wasn't even a traveler in this timeline? Maybe he just lived out his life like a regular person and knew the me from this timeline because we were neighbors.

My bus arrived and I had to sprint to my stop. I slipped into the nearest free seat two rows behind the driver. The bus rumbled along familiar roads, slowing to a stop every few blocks. I'd been spoiled by all my willing drivers in my own timeline. I'd never take them for granted again.

Nothing seemed to have changed as far as buildings and neighborhoods went. All the same shops in all the same places.

The bus pulled up in front of the school and I questioned myself again as to why I even bothered showing up. Would completing classes in this timeline show up as attendance in my own? If I just skipped out here, would I still appear to have attended classes and completed my homework in my own?

I had no idea. I only knew I couldn't afford to fail my senior year.

A girl waved to me from across the crowd. I couldn't miss that head of strawberry blond hair. Straight, sleek, golden locks like a princess out of a fairy tale—the complete opposite of my dark, flyaway curls. I flattened my expression, keeping the grimace that normally surfaced at the sight of Jessica Fuller at bay. If we really were friends in this timeline, I'd need her help.

"Hey," I said when I reached her.

"Hey. Why aren't you answering your texts?"

I did a double take at her accent and remembered to alter mine.

"Oh." I hadn't heard my phone chime. I removed it from my purse and saw several messages there, including a couple from Nate. "My ringer was off," I explained.

"I heard Nate's back from Australia?" she said. "You guys should come out with me and Austin tonight."

Her and Austin? Were they a thing?

"Yeah, maybe," I said. "Let me check with Nate."

The first bell rang and we joined the throng of bodies that snaked into the school. I quickly read my texts from Nate.

Nate: How are you feeling today?

Nate: Are you still sleeping?

Nate: Let me know you're okay, OK?

I was moved by his concern. I quickly texted him back.

Casey: I'm fine. My phone was off. Just heading to class now. Call you later.

As for what was becoming a regular problem, I didn't know where my locker was. Or which classes I was in when. I let Jessica take the lead, hoping she'd guide me. She stopped at a locker and leaned against it. I was guessing my locker was the one she was facing, right next to it. I tentatively reached for the lock and when Jessica didn't mock me, I tried my combo. The lock clicked open and I breathed out.

"What day is it?" I prompted. "I can't remember what class is next."

"Wow, did you have another bad night? It's English, prat."

130

Great. Our friendship was based on insults. Didn't really surprise me. And what did she mean by *another* bad night?

Austin snuck up from behind us and grabbed Jessica by the waist. She squealed and then threw herself in his arms, right in the middle of the hallway. I watched awkwardly as they kissed. No holding back on their PDA here! It was weird to see him with her like that, especially since *we* had been together recently in another timeline. It felt like they were blatantly rubbing their relationship in my face, which I knew was ridiculous. I stared at my shoes as I waited for them to detach. The main thing was I was back with Nate. I didn't care what Austin King did.

Austin finally separated from Jessica and disappeared down an adjoining hall.

"Wow," I said. "You guys are intense."

"You're blushing, Casey," Jessica said. "You're acting like you've never seen us snog before."

"It's just… nothing."

I hadn't seen Tim in the halls yet and scanned the faces as we walked.

Jessica noticed. "Who are you looking for?"

"Timothy."

"Timothy who?"

"My brother."

Jessica snorted. "What are you going on about?"

"I'm looking for my brother, Tim." It occurred to me then, that maybe Dad and Tim lived outside of Cambridge High boundary lines. Maybe Tim didn't even go to this school.

No wonder Jessica was looking at me so strangely.

"Unless you got big news last night you haven't told me about," she said, "you're still an only child."

Chapter Fifteen

I d experienced several versions of my family unit: Parents together, parents apart, brother as a Goth, injured but reformed, an arrogant jock.

But I'd never dreamed of the one I was faced with now. Father dead, brother never born.

This was the nutshell version I got out of a perplexed and impatient supposed best friend.

"Blimey, Casey, you're acting like you didn't know your dad passed on. You should see your face."

My blood flooded to my feet and I felt faint.

"I feel sick," I managed to say. I darted into the nearest bathroom and retched into the bathroom sink. Jessica followed me inside. "I told you not to eat that sushi yesterday. I mean, who eats raw fish? It's so barbaric."

133

I ignored her ignorant tirade. The only thing I could think of was that I was in a world where my brother and father didn't exist. Mom's overprotective statements made sense to me now.

There was no way I could accept this reality. I had to get back to my own, even if it meant Nate and I would never be together. I had to get my dad and brother back.

I cupped my hands, filled them with cool water, and slapped it gently to my face. Jessica leaned over the sink next to mine so she could get closer to her reflection in the mirror. She methodically applied lipstick to her lips and smacked them together. "Austin loves this color."

The door swung open and the girl who entered gasped at the sight of us. I gasped back. Instead of Lucinda's usually stylish flair, she wore plain ill-fitting clothes and her beautiful long hair had been cropped to her ears. Not a very flattering look on her. She froze momentarily before darting into one of the stalls. She actually looked frightened of us.

Jessica leaned up against the stall door and tapped. "Where's my essay?"

"I'm not doing that for you anymore."

"Really? I guess I'll be posting that special picture of you on Facebook, after all."

"Jessica," I said, feeling appalled. "Leave her alone."

Jessica shook her head. "Don't you get all weird on me now."

The second bell went and we were all good and late. "I'm skipping," Jessica said. "Wanna come?"

134

I shook my head. "Not this time."

"Fine." Jessica paused to take one more look at herself in the mirror. She still had her lipstick in her hand and wrote with a flourish on the mirror. "Lucinda is a Loser."

I recognized Jessica's big loopy letter "L" from when she wrote the same word on my locker in my sophomore year.

"I better have that report by Friday," Jessica said, before disappearing.

"Oh, God," I muttered. "I can't believe I'm friends with her."

"I can't believe it either." The toilet flushed and Lucinda exited her stall. She glared at me and then her gaze landed on Jessica's lipstick graffiti. I quickly wetted a paper towel and started to scrub it off.

"I'm really sorry about her," I said.

Lucinda turned on the taps and scoffed. "Since when?"

"Since whatever it was that happened to keep us from being friends."

"Just save it, Casey." She snapped paper towel out of the dispenser. "You know exactly what happened."

"No, really. I want to hear your side of the story."

I didn't think she'd stay but maybe she saw the grief and regret in my eyes. I wanted to know how it was possible for me to screw things up so terribly. What I could've done to make her hate me so much.

"The fall dance, sophomore year. We were supposed to go together. You really fancied Nate

135

Mackenzie, but he didn't know you existed. Jessica promised to set you up, all you had to do was ditch me as a friend. By the end of the dance, Jessica was with Austin and you were with Nate."

I couldn't believe I'd do something like that to Lucinda. But maybe I'd become a different person without Dad and Tim in my life. More selfish and self-centered, apparently.

"I'm sorry," I said.

She blinked in surprise. "You expect me to forgive you? While you're still blackmailing me?"

"I'm not blackmailing you." Or maybe I was. "Tell me what Jessica has on you, and I'll get it back."

"You know what she has."

"A picture," I said. Jessica had revealed that much. I had to guess Lucinda was caught in an unflattering situation. "Were you at a party?"

"*Yes*, I was at a party. I never go to parties, but I wanted to fit in. I drank too much and did something stupid. You know all that."

"You're not the only one to do something stupid at a party. What's the big deal?"

"The big deal is I need a scholarship if I want to go to college. A picture like that, once it's on the internet, never goes away. It'll ruin my reputation. No admissions counselor will let me in when they see it. Not to mention, my parents will kill me."

I knew all about compromising photos getting you into trouble.

"I'll get the picture back."

"How? Jessica has it on her phone."

"I'll find it and delete it for you. I promise."

"Why would you do that now? I don't understand?"

"People can change, Lucinda. I want to be your friend, and I'll do whatever I have to, to prove it to you."

"You chose *her* over me. We'd been inseparable since we were ten and you choose *a guy* over me."

The pain of betrayal etched across her face.

"I'm sorry," I said again. "I can't change what I did, but I can control what I do from now on."

Lucinda paused at the door before leaving. "Fine. Delete that photo. Then we'll talk."

I saw her again in the office where we were both picking up late slips. She didn't glance my way even once.

"This is your second tardy this week," the secretary said. "One more and you're in detention."

So, it seemed I made a habit of being late, too. I had a sneaking suspicion that my grades weren't all that great in this timeline either.

Somehow I made it through the day. Jessica guided me to most of my classes. I only had to beg one teacher for leniency when I arrived a half minute after the bell. I kept my eye on Jessica's purse, and the pocket where she kept her phone tucked away, but she never once parted from it, making it impossible to get access to it.

I met up with her after the last class of the day. "Nate and I would love to get together with you and Austin," I said with forced cheeriness. "What about tonight?"

She gaped. "On a school night?" Her eyes glimmered with her sarcasm. "You can break free from your mother?"

"My mom works late tonight," I said. It was a wild guess based on last night's timetable. Either way, I'd find a way to get out. I needed to delete that photo.

"I'll text you," Jessica said. Then she took off like a light out toward the parking lot. I could see Austin talking with a group of guys in the distance.

I just assumed I'd be taking the bus home, but then I caught sight of Nate's BMW. He honked when he spotted me.

I hopped into the passenger side and dropped my stuff by my feet. Nate leaned toward me and I felt a rush of euphoria. I needed Nate's hugs and kisses more than anything right now!

"Thanks for coming to get me," I said when I finally pulled myself away.

He grinned. "Believe me. It's my pleasure."

He drove out off school property and in the direction of my new home in the row house complex.

"Jessica invited us to hang out tonight with her and Austin."

Nate's jaw twitched. "Do we have to?"

"Just for a bit. She wants to hear about Australia."

I wanted to hear about Australia.

"Okay. But just for coffee. I know she's your friend, but she gets on my nerves."

"Just coffee," I agreed.

Nate had his iPod plugged into the old cassette player via an adapter, and turned up the music. I had the feeling we didn't actually talk much. I mean, he apparently just got home after being away in Australia for a month *and* gone to York University in Toronto for a semester, and he wasn't exactly talking my ear off. What was it that kept us together?

"Do you remember Willie Watson?" It was a test question. I didn't know for sure what it was this Nate actually knew about me and my second life.

He twisted his lips to one side. "Is he in your grade? Cuz, I don't really know that many people from Cambridge High, unless they were in my grad class."

"No, I just thought you might know him."

"Why is he a friend of yours?"

I hedged. Willie was a friend in a way I could never explain to Nate. It hurt me that we didn't share this vital part of my life. That he didn't know the family that was so much a part of how and where we had fallen in love.

"We're acquainted."

Nate didn't ask for more information and I didn't volunteer. The pit in my gut tightened. I didn't know this Nate. I didn't love him.

Chapter Sixteen

This version of my mom hadn't pursued her passion for interior design. It seemed her only passion was me. Our small home was neat as always, but no special effort to coordinate or keep with the trends. Instead there were many framed photos of me at various ages. A toddler on Santa's knee, eating cotton candy at a fair, riding a bike in this cul-d-sac. Had I actually grown up in this row house? It was weird seeing this other life another version of me had lived. It was like I was peeking in on the life of a long-lost identical twin.

I picked up a recent one of Nate and me. It was someone's birthday, if you could go by the cake and candles blurring in the background. I didn't remember this party. I had no memory of the photographer demanding us to smile.

Many of them were of me and Mom with our cheeks pressed together, her face gracefully aging over the years along with the maturation of mine. I got the sense it was the two of us against the world.

"I love looking at them, too."

I jumped at her voice.

"Yeah, they're great," I said.

Mom entered the living room with a bowl of popcorn in her hand. "Downton Abbey in five?" she said as she placed it on the coffee table.

"Actually, I'm going out for coffee with Nate, Jessica and Austin."

Mom's happy expression fell. "But, it's Thursday! We always watch Downton Abbey together on Thursday nights."

"But Nate just got back from Australia. He wants to show us pictures."

Mom worried her bottom lip and I wondered if she was actually going to forbid me to go. I was a senior in high school!

"Mom, I won't be out late. We can stream it later."

I was starting to understand why the other me tended to be a rebel.

Mom let out a reluctant sigh. "Okay, but be careful."

"I will. I'll be with Nate."

"And don't stay out late. Where are you going, exactly?"

"Dunkin's." The doorbell rang and I felt literally saved by it. Nate waited on the other side, hands in pockets standing in a relaxed posture.

"Hi, Mrs. Donovan," he said.

"Hi, Nate. Thanks again for picking Casey up yesterday." Her tone soured. "I was stuck at the office, and Casey would have to be in the hospital sick and dying before they'd let me leave early."

Nate's gaze cut to me then back to my mom. "It was no problem."

Her lips tightened and she shook her head. "I still don't know why her mates would've left her alone like that."

"It was a misunderstanding," I said. "All's well that ends well." I grabbed Nate's elbow. "We have to go. See you later, Mom."

I let out a breath when we finally closed the door and headed for Nate's car.

"Sorry about her," I said.

"It's fine," Nate said. "Maybe you should cut her some slack."

"Slack?"

"You know you're her whole world. She'll be gutted if you leave. Maybe you should reconsider your college choice?"

I slid into the passenger seat. "My college choice?" I said once Nate was inside the car. I was sounding like a parrot, but I needed him to give me clues.

"Yeah. You could go to Boston U, stay on campus if you really need to get away from here, but at least your mother wouldn't feel like you left her."

Where was I going if not to Boston U? "But I want to go…" Come on Nate, fill in the blank. Was I following him to Toronto now?

Nate shifted into reverse then draped his arm over the back of my seat as he twisted to look out the back window. "Everyone wants to go to New York, Case. But make sure it's what you really want to do. Don't go just to escape your mother."

I was going to college in New York? Which one? I didn't know how to get Nate to spit that detail out. I'd have to search my laptop. I was sure to have bookmarked the website or something.

He paused the car at the end of the drive and locked his eyes with mine. "Forget something?" I asked.

I studied his face. Everything I loved about it—the strong lines of his cheekbones and jawline, the still-water blue of his eyes. He leaned toward me and I met him in the middle.

Nate's lips were my absolute favorite and I was so happy to be kissing them again.

The photo of him and me together at an event I had no memory of flashed across my mind, jarring me. I felt like I was kissing Nate's twin, as if I were interloping in the love affair of another couple. I pulled away.

"Is something wrong? You've been off since I got back, and you still haven't explained what happened yesterday."

143

"I've been off?" Parrot, parrot!

"Yes. Subdued. Where'd my feisty Casey go? You're not still mad at me, are you?"

"Why would I be mad?"

"Because I went to Australia without you. I just couldn't wait until your summer break, you know. I have to work. Plus your mother would never forgive me if I spirited you away right now. I can tell you haven't forgotten our fights, but please, let's move on from this."

We fought over this? I couldn't go to Australia even if I wanted to. Maybe there was a version of Fiona in this scenario who went to York. Had she gone to Australia?

And how was *I* supposed to move on? Seriously??

Thankfully, the nearest Dunkin' Donuts was just around the corner and I could escape this conversation.

Jessica and Austin were already inside, snuggling together on one side of a booth. It kind of made me sick to my stomach.

Austin's wide shoulders were pressed into the window and he had one arm snaked over Jessica's shoulders. I motioned for Nate to enter the booth first, since I didn't want to be sitting across from Austin. I didn't want to make unnecessary eye contact. Maybe there was a part of his psyche that knew we'd kissed in another realm. Two other realms, actually. And that he was the reason I was in this big mess in the first place!

Jessica had ordered ahead and there were two coffees and two chocolate donuts sitting in front of Nate and me already. Nate tossed her a few bills. It felt like we'd done this double date before. I wondered if Nate and Jessica had dated before in this timeline. They seemed a little too comfortable.

Maybe I was just paranoid.

Jessica pushed the bills back across the table. "My treat. Welcome home."

"Yeah, welcome back dude," Austin added.

Nate had his phone out and scrolled through shots of iconic landmarks like the Sydney Harbour Bridge and the Sydney Opera House. And a lot of photos of the beach. I was starting to feel what the other me had felt: envy and disappointment. *I* wanted to have gone to Australia with Nate.

"That's brilliant!" Austin said. "Look at all those hot babes on the beach. Must've been hard to walk away from that!"

Jessica slapped his arm.

"Ouch! Why'd you do that?"

"Casey is right here." She wiggled away from his side. "*I'm* right here."

Austin grinned and tightened his hold. "I'm just kidding. You know you're the only one for me, Jessica."

He nibbled her ear.

I threw up a little in my mouth.

Jessica pushed out from the booth. "I gotta go to the loo."

I wanted to follow her, just to get away from being alone with both Nate and Austin, but I didn't want to be that girl that had to go to the restroom in pairs. Besides, Jessica left her purse on the floor under the table. This was

145

my chance to snag her phone and come through with my promise to Lucinda to delete that photo.

Austin and Nate talked sports while I surreptitiously worked to hook the strap of Jessica's purse with my toe. I carefully dragged it to my side of the table and lifted it up onto the seat. I was just about to slide my hand inside when Jessica popped up out of nowhere, scaring the heck out of me. I let out a little yelp.

"Oh, didn't mean to scare you," she said. Then her eyes landed on the black bag on my lap. "I forgot my purse."

"Yes," I answered quickly. "I was just about to bring it to you."

"Well, hand it over."

I delivered her purse and then grabbed mine. Who cared if we were going to the restroom in twos.

"Be right back," I said to Nate. I hadn't given up on my mission to delete the offending photo and hoped Jessica would provide me with another chance.

"What's the scoop with you and Nate?" Jessica said as we walked down the hall.

I pushed on the bathroom door. "What do you mean?"

"You seem very stand-offish. I know he's been gone a lot, but it looks like things between you have really cooled."

"Oh, well, it is strange," I admitted. "Lots of time away can change people."

"You were so crazy for him, but I get it." She disappeared behind a stall door. "I'm going to break up with Austin."

"What?" I'd never guess that by the way they'd been fawning over each other. "Why?"

"We're going to different colleges." The toilet flushed and Jessica exited the stall and began to wash her hands. "We want different things in life. Is that what you're thinking?"

"I guess."

"You know, we should break up with them now."

"Now?"

"Yeah, band-aid it. Why take the time to get used to Nate being around again just so you have a date for the dance?"

Jessica's thought processes were moving at the speed of light. I could barely keep up. "It'd be nice to have someone to take us to the dance."

"This is the twenty-first century, Casey. We don't need a guy to take us anywhere. We can just *go*. You and me, we'll go together."

"As dates?"

"No." She rolled her eyes like I was really slow on the uptake. And I was, apparently. "As singles. The whole point is to go to the dance *without* dates."

She finished applying lipstick and drew a brush through her hair. The direction the conversation had taken totally derailed my delete-Lucinda's-photo mission.

"Can I borrow your phone?" I said. "I forgot mine and I promised my mom I'd call."

147

"I'm surprised she hasn't gotten your ear tattooed like a dog. Some kind of GPS chip so she could always track you. I don't blame you for wanting to go to NYU. I'd go crazy if my mother smothered me like that."

She handed me her phone and disappeared out the door.

I searched Jessica's photo app and found a couple of Lucinda getting sick into a toilet. Delete. Delete.

Then I called my mom. "We're still at Dunkin's but will be home soon."

There was an audible sigh from her end. "Smashing. Thanks for letting me know you're safe, pumpkin. I'll make fresh popcorn."

I wondered if Jessica was serious about us breaking up with our boyfriends tonight. I wasn't sure how I felt about it. How would Casey from this timeline feel? I didn't want to screw things up for her.

Chapter Seventeen

Turned out, I didn't have a chance to find out. A wave of dizziness hit me hard and I fell through a tunnel of light.

Slowly.

The light fractured into a brilliant rainbow swirl—yellow, green, blue, indigo. I felt it on my skin, at times slick and slippery like oil and others smooth like satin.

I fell as if caught in space, floating weightless. My heart beat in my ears. Tripping had never taken more than a few seconds before. Was I trapped in this funnel of light? How badly had I screwed things up?

Thudump, thudump.

Fear rattled my rib cage. I grabbed for my heart, but my arms were frozen, paralyzed. I let out a silent scream.

And then suddenly, I was on my feet. The world around me was dark, and I let out a gasp. Was I now *blind?*

"Casey?"

I turned sharply towards the familiar voice. "Paul Junior?"

I startled by his hand on my arm. "I can't see!"

"It's all right," Paul Junior whispered. "Your eyes will adjust in a few moments."

As he spoke the words, the blackness around me lightened to gray. I could make out Paul Junior's silhouette. A thicker-built figure moved into view. Paul Revere? I searched the horizon and blinked at the tiny bug-like lights reflecting off a watery surface.

I was back to the moment before Paul Revere launched his ill-fated canoe into the Charles River. I'd tripped from Cambridge to Boston. I'd never tripped from one location to another. It was always the same piece of land, just a new era. Time always moved along in the past before too, but here I was, back to the exact moment I'd left.

How was this possible? It broke all the time-travel laws! I wanted to scream. None of the rules seem to apply anymore. I had no safety net.

"Casey," Paul Junior said. "You're trembling."

"I'm sorry. I'm just…"

"You're wearing men's clothes."

I wore the clothes I had on at Dunkin Donuts. Jeans, a long spring cardigan and sneakers. I rubbed my sweaty hands on my thighs.

"Paul Junior," Paul Revere whispered. "I need your assistance."

I blurted, "You have to change boats!"

Paul Junior put a finger to my lips. "Shh. The Regulars will hear you."

I pointed to Paul Revere. "You must get another one."

My eyes had fully adjusted to the darkness now, and I could see the look of exasperation on Paul Revere's face.

"There's no time," he said.

"That canoe will sink." He shot me a bewildered look.

Paul Junior's eyes flashed with understanding as he scanned my new wardrobe for a second time. "Pa, we should listen to her. There's another in the boathouse. We can retrieve it quickly."

Paul Revere hesitated, "Why?"

"I can't explain," Paul Junior said, "but I'm asking you to trust me."

Paul Revere let out a long breath, then broke into a jog inland.

"I'll help," I said.

Paul Junior and I raced after him, through the wiry bushes. Branches scraped across my face, got caught on my clothes and scratched my hands, but I didn't care. I pushed on after Paul Junior until we approached the small wooden shed. This outbuilding had probably been built in a clearing, but over time the trees and brush had overrun it until a footpath was the only indication something existed

151

here. Paul Revere had the doors wide open and I stepped into the dark damp, moldy-smelling place.

The Revere men knew the space and found what they were looking for easily in the dark. They each took one end of a second canoe and flipped the heavy boat onto their shoulders, groaning a little under the weight. I crouched underneath the middle section and stood, bearing the weight on my hands above my head.

We clumsily wormed our way back to the shore, and I felt particularly handicapped. Once again I was blinded, this time by my position, and often caught my toe on exposed roots and sharp rocks.

Finally the river song grew louder and the soil beneath our careful steps, softer. We hoisted the boat to the sand and I stretched out in relief. My arms and shoulders burned. I'd be sore in the morning.

We remained silent as we carefully maneuvered the replacement vessel into the river. Paul Junior and I steadied the boat while Paul Revere climbed in with his paddles in hand. He situated himself on the middle bench, then saluted us. Paul Junior and I saluted back. It was a long way to Cambridge by canoe, and his journey would take him dangerously close to the enemy war ship. A pretty brave move by someone who couldn't swim.

I wondered if the time lost by switching canoes would make a difference. Would Paul Revere deliver the message to Lexington and Concord in time? Would America be America again?

When Paul Revere disappeared from view, Paul Junior and I picked up the faulty boat and dragged it to the boathouse.

When we were safely away from shore, Paul Junior asked, "How did you know it had a leak?"

"I've lived through this scenario once before," I said.

Paul Junior nodded. "I thought so. Your sudden change in wardrobe, though shocking, was convincing."

We left the boat in the shed, upside down. "I'll come in the morrow to make repairs," Paul Junior said.

Now that our mission was accomplished, my adrenaline surge plummeted and I was hit with a wall of fatigue.

Paul Junior nudged my elbow. "Let's go home."

We trudged through the darkness and more than once I had to grab Paul Junior's sleeve to keep from falling on my face. My mind scampered to catch up to the turn of events. One moment Nate and I were double-dating with Jessica and Austin and the next I was re-aligning American history.

My relational troubles with Nate, or the many versions of Nate, made me think of Paul Junior's sister. "How's Deborah?"

Paul Junior shrugged. "You were there when I saw her last."

Right. It felt like ages ago to me, but was only a few hours for Paul Junior.

"I think it was very courageous of her to go against her heart to support the colonies."

Elle Strauss

"Courage wouldn't have been required if she had not secretly met with him in the first place."

"Well, at least she did the right thing. She gave them false information which will help to scatter their army, at least a little."

I stumbled over the cobblestones and Paul Junior grabbed my hand. Before I could straighten fully, I was slapped with bright, white light.

Panic gripped me as awareness dawned—that I had Paul Junior's hand in mine, which meant he was coming with me, *wherever* and *whenever* that might be!

Chapter Eighteen

Paul Junior and I stood on the steps of Marlene Charter's brownstone, me in crusty river-water jeans and scuffed up jacket and Paul Junior in worn dungarees tucked into tall leather boots and a loose white shirt.

I held a red ladder-back chair in one hand.

I gently set it down on the sidewalk one step down and took a seat.

"Was it you or me?" I asked.

Paul Junior bent over to untuck his pants from his boots. He tried to brush out the wrinkles along his shins without much success. "It was me," he said. "I felt it come on, just as I reached to assist you. I suppose it's for the best, that I was able to bring you home."

He scrutinized my appearance—my not-so-twenties apparel and my wild, wind-blown mass of loose curls. "Except this is not your home, is it?"

I shook my head. "I haven't been 'home' for a while, Paul Junior." I felt tears of defeat burn behind my eyes. "I broke something major. The laws of time travel are messed up."

"Is your home a long time from now?"

I nodded. "Yeah. And a really long time from your home."

"Two hundred years?"

"Two hundred and forty."

Paul Junior whistled.

The wind picked up, almost as if his whistle brought it on, and our attention was drawn to a wide slapping sound above. A flag.

Despite my weariness, I smiled. The stars and stripes fluttered proudly.

Paul Junior followed my gaze. "Looks like my father made it."

"Yeah." I stood and picked up the chair. "I guess I better get this to Marlene."

"And I should go as well." He held out a hand. I hesitated before taking it, not wanting to accidentally tag along on another of Paul's trips, but I doubted one would happen so soon afterward. I gave his hand a good shake.

"You take care," I said. I had no way of knowing if our paths would cross again. There was a good chance we'd never see each other again.

"You too, Casey. It was a pleasure and an honor to meet you."

"Likewise, Paul Junior."

I watched him saunter off until he disappeared around the corner with one last wave and a crooked grin. I smoothed out my shirt in a vain attempt to prepare myself for what awaited inside. I scrambled for a story that could explain the way I was dressed, and finally gave up. I might as well just face Marlene and Lolly and take whatever they dished out, probably in the form of scorn and mockery.

I eased the door open and stepped inside. Marlene and Lolly were sitting at the kitchen table, their backs to me, drinking coffee and smoking cigarettes.

"Maybe you should just let Sheldon go, darling," Lolly said, tapping ashes into a tray. "He's no good for you. And you don't need him. Look at you! Already rich with all your stocks."

Marlene pulled hard on her cigarette and let out a long plume of smoke out of the side of her mouth. "Not rich enough to leave Ma."

"Not yet, maybe, but soon. And if you insist on dancing at illegal establishments, there's plenty more around not owned by the Vance brothers."

Marlene's eyes widened and her mouth dropped open.

"What?" Lolly said. "Ya think I didn't know how you were making all that cash?"

Marlene circled her cigarette in the air. "What about you and Thomas Burgess? Are you finally gonna stand up to *your* Ma?"

I'd been leaning on the back of the chair and the legs finally shifted from my weight, scraping across the floor. The girls turned and gawked.

"Hey," I said. "I bought you a new chair."

Lolly frowned. "What are you wearing? What happened to my mother's dress?"

"Oh, about that." I smiled sheepishly. "I don't think I can explain."

"You are the oddest bird!" Marlene said. She turned to Lolly. "Jeepers creepers! How ever did we get mixed up with her?"

Lolly butted out her cigarette and said to Marlene, "She's harmless." To me she added, "Would you like a coffee? You're looking a little peaked."

"I'd love a glass of water, actually." I sat in one of the empty chairs and rested my arms and my head on the table. I was so wiped out, I couldn't even pretend to pretend anymore.

"If you're gonna keep dropping by with unexplainable fashion sense and style, could you at least bring that handsome beau with you?"

I peeked up at her. "Nate?"

She popped a couple smoke rings. "Yes, Nate."

"We're not together anymore. You won't see him again."

Marlene smirked. "Well, maybe not with you around."

Ah, 'k, whatever. Lolly returned with a tall glass of water and I gulped it back. I hadn't had a drop to drink since the double date, and since that time I'd hauled two canoes around and traipsed across Boston in the dark.

"Thanks, Lolly." I wiped my face with the back of my hand.

Marlene shot me a look of disgust and blew smoke in my face. I made a scene by flapping my hand and waving it away.

Marlene ignored me and hopped to her feet. "Let's go shopping! All this cleaning is making me grumpy." She butted out her cigarette with a flourish. "I'll go change into something more presentable. I'll be back in a jiffy."

Lolly sat across from me and scrutinized me with a look of concern. "What happened to you between here and the hardware store?"

I sighed. She wouldn't believe me if I tried to explain. I just shrugged and decided to turn the attention back to her.

"What about that Thomas Burgess?" I didn't know if Lolly's choice of a husband affected my timeline anymore or not. I didn't even know if I'd ever get back to my timeline at this rate, but I thought it wouldn't hurt to bring it up one more time, just in case.

Lolly sat back. "What about him?"

"I think he's nice. And he likes you."

She scrunched her nose. "How do you know that?"

"I can tell by how he looks at you when you're not paying attention."

Lolly let out a little huff. "I don't know. Maybe."

Marlene skipped down the stairs. She wore a classic shimmering flapper dress with long beads and shin-length frills. Her face was made up heavily and she wore a black sparkly headband over her bob of finger waves. Marlene liked to make a splash wherever she went, day or night.

She shot perfume in the air and I almost choked on the sudden sweetness.

"Ma hates when I smoke in the house," she explained.

Lolly stood and gathered her things. "Are you coming?"

I shook my head. "Would you mind if I stayed behind? I'm not up to it."

Marlene rolled her eyes. "Fine. We'll see you later."

They shut the door behind them with a bang and I soaked in the peace and quiet left in their wake. Maybe I'd lie down on the sofa for a while. I was so exhausted.

I took two strides from the kitchen to the living room, not quite making it to the sofa before I was hit by a wave of dizziness. I fell through the light with no idea what to expect next and quite glad that Marlene and Lolly had left before I disappeared into thin air.

160

Chapter Nineteen

I should've run outside! I knew better! Now I was standing in front of two pre-teen boys with controllers in their hands and shocked expressions on their faces.

One exclaimed, "Whoa!"

The other sang, "How'd you do that?"

The room was decorated with contemporary furnishings and the big flat screen attached to the wall over a gas fireplace was a good indication that I was back to my own time.

"Sorry to interrupt boys," I said, "but I gotta go."

Outside I was relieved to find the twenty-first century Boston clustered with concrete high-rises. I wanted to fall to the ground and kiss the sidewalk. I'd made it home!

I didn't have a phone, or money for transit, and I was too tired to deal with my latest predicament, feeling completely whiplashed by all the time-travel I'd been doing lately.

I waved down a cab, praying that there would be someone at my house who could pay the fare.

The rumble of the taxi lulled me instantly to sleep and before I knew it the cabby was calling for me.

"Lady? We're here. Lady?"

My eyes flickered as I worked to make sense of the fact that I was toppled over onto the grimy backseat of a cab, adding my slobber to the grossness. I pushed myself upright and stared out at my house. A flat-faced white colonial with black wooden shutters. A manicured yard. A screened in porch.

Yay! It was my house! "I'll be right back," I said excitedly. "I just have to go inside to get your money."

I hopped out before the cabbie could protest. Just as I approached the front door, Tim walked out. And he was limping! (Which on its own wasn't something I'd celebrate, but it confirmed I was back in my own time line.)

"Tim!" I was so relieved to see him. I hadn't forgotten the time I spent in a world where he hadn't existed and how sad and hollow I'd felt.

I threw myself at him and gave him the biggest bear hug ever! "It's so good to see you!" Now that I'd experienced life without him in it, I was overjoyed and hugged him extra hard.

He shook me off and deep scowl lines formed on his face. "Get off me! What's your problem?"

Right. For him, nothing had changed. I felt like I'd lived through a dozen lifetimes but as far as Tim was concerned he'd just seen me that morning at breakfast.

Still, he wasn't usually so brusque with me.

"Is something wrong?" I asked.

"Only the way you're acting so weird." He shifted his weight and brushed past me and I watched his familiar uneven gait as he shuffled down the street.

Maybe he was having girl problems, or a teacher had come down on him hard. I'd talk to him later at home when I could keep my gleeful outbursts under control.

The cabbie beeped his horn, and I waved to let him know I was on it.

I sprinted to my room and searched the drawer where I often kept extra cash. Thankfully there were bills there, enough for the fare and a tip. It pretty much emptied the drawer out, but I didn't care about that at this point. The cabbie was thankful.

Inside the house was exactly as it should be, all the same furnishings and wall hangings, everything with Mom's special design flare. I skipped and squealed. It was so good to be back!

"Mom!" I waited for her response from the top of the stairs, but it was quiet. Her office was empty. A cursory check of the house and garage proved she wasn't home. I felt a wash of disappointment.

I grabbed an apple off the kitchen counter and crunched into it, slurping its juiciness. I was famished and gnawed it to the core. It was only when I tossed the remains into the compost pail under the sink that I noticed the note by the phone.

Casey and Tim,

Dad and I will be gone until the weekend. There's food in the fridge to last you until then.

Mom

I scrunched up my face in confusion. Where had they gone? I didn't remember a planned getaway. I couldn't even remember the last time my parents went away together.

I searched the fridge as Mom had suggested and made myself a sandwich. Then I headed upstairs for a shower and finally, to sleep.

I awoke to honking and my phone by my bed buzzing.

Lucinda's name flashed at me.

"Hey?" I said sleepily.

"Casey!"

"Hi, Lucinda. I slept in."

"Well get your butt in gear. I'll come in. I know where the key is."

I had to bite my lip to keep from smiling like a drowsy lunatic. We were friends again! After all the timeline jumping I'd been doing, it was just so good to be *back*.

I roused myself out of bed and into the bathroom. By the time I'd finished washing my face and brushing my teeth, Lucinda was in my room sitting on my bed. She wore trendy jeans and a lacy blouse with cute shoes and a matching purse. Her dark brown hair ran long and sleek down her back. I smiled at her. She looked great! Such a change from the version of her where her self-esteem had been stomped into the ground.

She wore more makeup than I was used to seeing on her—maybe she was meeting up with Sam again. She popped in a piece of chewing gum.

"Hey, " I said trying to keep it cool. I didn't want to freak her out like I had Tim by giving her the bear hug I so wanted to do. Instead I dug through my closet and got dressed.

Lucinda snapped her gum. "I suppose one more late slip before grad's not gonna kill us."

"Sorry about that. I forgot to set my alarm."

"It's fine. Hey, I know I keep reminding you of this, but now it's only nineteen days until the prom," she said. "Has anyone asked you yet?"

Oh, Right. The Prom. No one had asked me because here, Nate and I had only recently split up. There was still a chance that we could get back together. Slim but possible, and I found myself harbouring hope.

Lucinda took my silence to mean no and continued. "Obviously, I'm going to the dance with Sam."

I ran a brush through my hair. "So things with Sam are going well?"

"Of course. Why wouldn't they be?"

I shrugged. They'd only just gotten together, but whatever. I chose a pair of flats—I owned a number because I was tall and already towered above all of the girls and some of the guys.

"And Jessica's going with Nate…"

"Wait! What??" I screeched. My throat withered dry and I could hardly swallow. "Jessica and Nate?"

Lucinda's brow buckled as threw me an odd look. "Yes, Jessica and Nate. Earth to Casey? What's the matter with you? Are you stressed because *you* don't have a date to the dance yet? What about Austin King? I think he likes you."

I pinched my eyes closed and lowered myself to the floor. Nate wasn't supposed to be with Jessica. Maybe with Floozy, but not Jessica.

Unless this wasn't my timeline.

My insides turned to mush. This wasn't my timeline!

"Casey? You could ask Austin, you know. Girls are allowed to do that."

"No! I'm not asking Austin to the dance."

"Why? What's wrong with him?"

"Nothing. Nothing's wrong with him." I cupped my face with my hands and breathed. I felt hyperventilation coming on. "I don't think I'm going to go."

"Of course you're going. Don't be stupid. Look, if you're not interested in Austin, I'm sure Sam could hook you up with one of his friends. But you have to go to the prom, Casey." Her voice took on a pouty tone. "It would be so weird for you not to be there. Kindergarten to grad, you and me."

I glanced up at her. She sat on the edge of the bed, her brown eyes wide and pleading. I was still her best friend in this realm and I should be there for her.

"Okay, I'll go. But I don't need a date."

"Won't that be a little strange?"

"No, why should it? It's the twenty-first century. Girls don't need guys to go anywhere." I couldn't believe I was quoting Jessica Fuller. A version of Jessica Fuller.

Lucinda grinned. "That's very girl-power of you."

Whatever. I'd go the stupid dance, but I didn't see a reason to go to school. This wasn't my time-line after all. I literally felt sick.

"You know, Lucinda, my stomach's off."

"Actually, you don't look that great. Maybe that's why you slept in. You're probably fighting something."

"Yeah, I think I'll just go back to bed. I'm sorry I made you late for school."

Lucinda stood and reached out a hand to help me up. *My* Lucinda would never do that. She'd grab my elbow or reach under my arm, anything but purposefully touch my skin. I pretended not to see her and jumped to me feet on my own. I made up for my slight by giving her a hug.

"Okay, bye Casey. Call me later."

"I will."

She disappeared and I heard her footsteps pad down the carpeted stairwell. When the front door closed, I took a quick look around the house for Tim. I assumed he'd left for school, but I just wanted to make sure I was home alone before I let myself fully engage in my pity party.

167

All clear.

The tears escaped and I searched for a tissue. I went back to my room and crawled into bed.

I couldn't take this anymore. Was this my life now? Back and forth from the eighteenth century (or was it the twentieth now?) to an always changing present timeline? Was I destined to live out my days on this time travel slinky?

My chest heaved as a billow of air escaped my lungs followed by a guttural groan. I pinched back my tears and covered my face with my damp palms. I was stuck. What was the point? Who cared if I went to school or graduated? Who cared if Nate continued to break my heart, one way or another? Who cared if my best friend constantly had a different boyfriend or that I was still apparently friends with Jessica Fuller? Who cared!!

And once again, I had no one to share my troubles with.

Or, maybe I did. Tim was wounded, and that injury happened on a time travel loop. Could I confide in this version of him? Would he understand? Better yet, would he be able to help?

But how? I couldn't think of a scenario where that could be the case.

I spent most of the day in bed with one break from my depression to eat a bowl of cereal.

Lucinda texted sometime after lunch.

Lucinda: Hey. Jessica and I are going dress shopping for the prom after school. Are you feeling better? You should come.

I chortled. The irony! Maybe Nate would be there too, at Filenes, and I could knock over a rack of dresses or something.

Casey: I'm still pretty sick. I wouldn't want you guys to catch anything.

Lucinda: Too bad. Oh well. I'll keep a look out for something for you. I'll text you with photos. Feel better!

How could I feel better when my BFF was BFF with my nemesis? Ugh. I made an unavoidable trip to the bathroom to relieve myself. I tried not to look in the mirror when I washed my hands, but it was hard to miss the puffiness and bloodshot tint in my eyes. And I had a bedhead nest of curls fit to house a family of mice.

I crawled back into bed, pulling the covers up to my chin and curled into a ball. I'd be happy to spend the rest of my life here. Maybe I would.

Another hour passed before I heard someone enter through the front door below.

Irregular footsteps sounded on the stairs and I propped myself up on my elbows. "Tim!"

The footsteps grew closer and I called for my brother again. "Tim!"

He pushed on my door. "What's up?"

"Come in for a minute."

"In your room?"

"Yeah." He was acting like he'd never hung out with me in my room before. I waved to my desk chair. "Have a seat."

He shrugged. "Okay, but make it quick."

169

"How's the leg?" I asked.

Tim frowned. "Still gimpy."

Gimpy? I'd never heard Tim use that word before. Not in relation to his injury anyway.

I waited for him to ask me questions. I was demonstrating classic return-from-a-trip behaviour. *My* Tim would ask me about it. This one didn't. How did he get the leg injury then? How do I ask about something I should already know? This kind of situation was becoming a major problem for me.

I motioned to his leg. "Does it hurt all the time?"

Tim shrugged. "Just where the bullet destroyed nerve and muscle tissue."

The bullet. But not a musket, so what then?

I tried an open-ended lead. "Did they find..."

"Find what? The guy who robbed the bank? Believe me. You'd know if they did."

"Robbed the bank?" Parroting was apparently my modus operandi.

"Man, Casey, you're acting like you weren't even there."

I was there. But in my timeline, Officer Porter took the bullet, not Tim.

"Sorry. I'm kind of out of it. I must've dreamed that they found the guy."

"Yeah, whatever." Tim stood and limped away without another word to me.

I let my head fall to my pillow feeling completely defeated and so alone with my ginormous problems.

I rolled onto my back, and spent an hour or so re-evaluating my situation. Maybe there was something I could do. I sat up with renewed purpose. There was one person who might be able to help me.

Chapter Twenty

My confidence wavered as I got of the bus at the townhouse community I'd lived in with my mother in another timeline. I watched a small boy play in the front yard of the unit I'd called my home for a short while. I remembered clearly how lost I felt as I fished out the key from under the gnome and watched with a hollow pit in my stomach as Nate drove away.

The gnome was missing.

I hadn't come back to reminisce.

I walked passed the small boy, finger waving and offering a smile. He ran into the house and I thought for a moment he was going to call for his mother and I'd come off looking like a would-be child snatcher. I picked up my pace and crossed the street.

I stopped when I reached #24 and stared nervously at the front door. Maybe this wasn't a good idea. This Samuel probably wasn't a traveler. He probably didn't know who I was—who I *really* was.

I didn't think I could bear that.

I almost spun on my heels and walked away when the door inched open. Samuel's brown, wrinkled face broke into a smile. "Casey Donovan. Are you going to come in?"

I hesitated, then said, "Yes, thank you."

Samuel's home was much the same as the one in my time. Simply furnished with a couple easy chairs and a sofa in the living room. A plain kitchen table with four chairs in the dining area.

He even had a similar-looking cat. "What's its name?"

His eyes sparkled. "Willie."

"Willie?" I was hoping he'd say Watson. That was the cat's name in my timeline. It was nod toward the Watson family, the people both Samuel and I had stayed with when we tripped to the 1860s.

Willie was a common name, especially for a pet, but it was also the name of the eldest Watson son.

"It was either that or Watson," he said, grinning, answering the question he must've read on my face.

I grinned back feeling like a load just fell off my shoulders.

"Tea?" he asked. "I have a feeling we have a long visit ahead of us."

I nodded. "Sounds great."

Samuel's kitchen was small with U-shaped counters. He boiled the water in an electric kettle and poured it over tea bags he'd plopped into a teapot. He placed that on a tray, along with two teacups, milk and sugar and a small package of sugar cookies.

"I'll carry it," I offered, then followed him with the tray back to the living room.

Samuel poured the tea. "Milk and sugar?" he said, more like he was confirming what he knew than asking something he didn't know. I nodded.

We settled into our respective, slightly worn, armchairs. Willie the cat hopped on Samuel's lap and Samuel stroked him behind the ears.

"He looks like a good companion," I said.

"I like him."

The room was plain but cozy. There was a fireplace against the far wall, and I imagined it was really nice in the winter.

"So, Casey. What brings you to this fine neighborhood?"

"You do. I have a lot to tell you, and I have a problem of sorts, that I'm hoping you can help me with."

Samuel leaned his easy chair back and put his feet up. "I'm always ready for a good story. Please begin."

I blew on my tea and took a little sip to ease my dry mouth. I was nervous. This Samuel was playing it cool, but I was about to dump a major tale on him. My first sentence was sure to rock him.

"I've altered time."

Samuel blinked but other than that his expression remained staid. "Go on."

"This isn't my timeline. I screwed it up. I shouldn't be here," I said quickly. "I made a huge mistake, a fifteen on a scale of one to ten, and now I'm here, but I belong in another timeline and I don't know how to get back."

Samuel's expression grew alarmed. "Now, now, slow down. Why don't you start from the beginning?"

I took a deep breath and told myself to slow down. "I started falling back into time when I was ten years old. I always went back to the same time and place. I mean, time there moved on, but in relation to actual time. More or less. I had the same loop to the 1860s. That's where I met you."

I paused to take a sip of my tea, my eyes staying on his deep brown ones. "I did meet you there, didn't I?"

"Let's stick to your story for now."

"Okay. I tripped back and forth, semi-regularly, but nothing ever changed in my own timeline as a result. My reasoning was that whatever happened in the past had already happened in my present, even if I hadn't factually gone back to the past yet. It was a weird life of duality, but I managed it. I had friends, the Watsons, who helped me out there. My own family and friends didn't even know— well, my brother eventually found out, and my best friend knows and my boyfriend, er, former boyfriend—and you, but no one else. I imagined going through my whole life this way."

Samuel reached for one of the sugar cookies. "What happened to change that?"

"I did something extremely stupid. Nate, do you know Nate?" I waited for Samuel to react, but he just waved his fingers for me to continue. "Nate is my boyfriend. *Was* my boyfriend. He goes to Boston University. I'm still a senior in High school. I've always been nervous about college girls because Nate is really good-looking and athletic. Anyway, we went a long time without seeing each other and there was this girl, Fiona, who was after him, and I was insecure, and jealous, because they were going to Spain together, well not together, but they were both going to Spain, and I hated that I couldn't go. Because, you know, I didn't want to trip over the Atlantic.

"So I went to Hollywood instead. Even though it still involved flying, I could *sleep* through it, and it was a risk, maybe a dumb risk, but I was angry and hurt and I *needed* to do it, you know?

"Except there was this guy, Austin King, who decided that he was interested in me. Just like Fiona was interested in Nate. Ugh! Such a big soap opera!

"He showed me a picture that *looked* like Nate kissing Fiona, but he wasn't. Except that I *did* kiss Austin. Because I'm such an idiot!

"I was so upset, I triggered a trip. I ran away and straight into Adeline Savoy."

I had to stop because I felt a whoosh of dizziness. I feared momentarily I was about to trip but then realized it was just that I was on the verge of hyperventilating. I took a long pull of my now tepid tea.

"Who's Adeline?"

Samuel finished his second cookie and wiped crumbs off his chin. Willie purred contentedly on his lap.

"She's another traveler. I'd met her briefly in Cambridge a couple of years ago, and then we met up in Hollywood. I know, small world! So, she was at the same party, and just happened to be having a fight with her boyfriend, which triggered a trip for her. We ran into each other, literally."

Samuel put up a hand. "Don't tell me. You tripped together while touching skin to skin."

"Yes! Have I told you this story before?" I wondered if there had been another timeline I didn't remember where I'd discussed this change of event already. That would mean Samuel didn't—or couldn't—help me. I slumped lower in my chair.

"No, you didn't tell me this already. I'm a good guesser."

I filled him in on everything that had happened since Hollywood 1929 right up to the latest venture in 1775 and getting Paul Revere into the canoe.

Willie stretched on Samuel's lap before springing to the floor. Samuel threaded his hands over a comfortable belly. "You do have a big problem."

"I know! What can I do to stop this? Please, Samuel! There must be something?"

He squinted at me. "What makes you think I can help you?"

"Can't you?" I covered my face with my hands. "Of course you can't! You don't trip anymore. You don't have magic powers. What was I thinking?"

It was hopeless. I didn't know why I thought Samuel could help me. He was just like me and I couldn't help myself. My distress manifested itself in leaky eyes and nose. I wiped my face on my sleeve in a very unladylike manner.

Samuel pulled a tissue from his sweater pocket and handed it to me. I registered that it was clean as I accepted it. "Thank you," I said with a little hiccup.

"Now, now, dear. I didn't say I couldn't help you. I was just curious about what you thought I could do."

"Can you help me?"

"Possibly."

"How?"

Samuel leaned forward, placing his pointy elbows on bony knees. "Would you like to go for a ride?"

Oh. Nice change of subject. "Sure. Where to?"

"I'll show you."

Samuel eased carefully out of his chair like old men do and headed for the front door. I jumped up and followed him.

Fresh spring air filled my lungs, pleasantly warm for this time of year. We caught the first bus to the train station, then hopped on the T to Somerville. We chose two empty seats together. A young hipster couple across from us had their heads together as they watched something on a tablet in the guy's hand. They chuckled quietly. They were so cute together and obviously comfortable with each other. My heart whinged with envy and I had to look away.

Samuel cleared his throat, then spoke quietly. "Do you notice that you have certain triggers—stress elements that proceed a travel episode?"

I nodded. "Yes. Stress in all forms does it for me. Stress causing tripping causes stress causes tripping. Or at least it used to. I'm in a terrible cycle."

Samuel hummed with understanding. "Think of time travelling like you're playing in strong ocean waves. The energy of the ocean pulls you under and spits you out according to its own whim. The swimmer is at nature's mercy."

"That's exactly what it's like! I feel tossed about and without anchor."

"The human mind is a powerful thing, Casey. Your brain is a mass of neurons and synapses in constant motion. Like the ocean, you can't tame it but you can ride it."

"Like a surfer?"

"Precisely."

I arched a brow and leaned closer. "Are you saying you can control your trips?"

Samuel pushed out his lips and gave me a slight nod. "It took some research and a lot of trial and error, but like you, I was tired of being thrown about the rocks."

His comment surprised me. "I didn't think it was an issue for you anymore. I thought you stopped travelling."

"Why did you think that?"

Because the Samuel I knew from my own timeline had. I shrugged a shoulder. "No reason."

179

The train stopped at our destination and we exited near a strip mall. I started to clue in. In 1863 this was the site next door to the Watsons' farm.

I pondered Samuel's reference to surfing time and stared hard at him. "You can go back there, at will?"

He offered a humble shrug. "Usually."

"Really! And you'd take me back? Would that…." My mind raced. "Would that reset my time loop?" If I could get back to the timeline I belonged in, maybe I could get home.

I held in my desire to squeal. I didn't want Samuel to see how eager I was, no, how desperate I was. I couldn't risk scaring him off, that'll he'd become afraid of disappointing me or something.

"There's only one way to find out," Samuel said. "Care for some tea?"

Chapter Twenty—One

His sudden change of topic confused me, but I complied. "Sure. I'm kind of thirsty."

There was a teashop run by a hippie couple in the strip mall. A bell rang over the door when we walked in and we were immediately hit with a myriad of floral and spicy tea scents.

"What would you like, Casey?" Samuel asked. "My treat."

I'd like to trip all the way back to the Watsons and restart my loop, thank you very much. "Strawberry tea would be nice."

The server scooped actual tea leaves into a silver tea ball that hooked onto the side of our tea cups and presented two small teapots of hot water. Samuel paid, and I carried our drinks to the nearest empty table.

We went through the ritual of placing the tea balls into the teapots and waited the few minutes necessary to properly steep. I swirled my tea ball around impatiently. I knew Samuel wouldn't talk until our tea was ready.

Instrumental music piped in on a low volume along with the pleasant hum of customer chatter filled the small tea room. I poured my tea into my cup and added milk. Samuel did the same. After my first sip I asked, "Why are we drinking tea?"

Samuel carefully placed his teacup into his saucer. "The act of drinking tea naturally puts you into a calmer state of mind."

"Are you saying, all this time I could've been controlling my travels if I'd just been drinking *tea?*"

Samuel chortled. "Getting relaxed helps, but you need to funnel your brain energy yourself. Visualize yourself surfing time."

I almost snorted. He couldn't be serious. A thought crossed my mind that maybe *this* Samuel *was* crazy. If I was still tripping as a senior citizen, I was sure I'd be crazy too.

"I'm not crazy," he said.

What? He was a mind reader now?

"Relaxation, visualizing and this…" He pulled a small packet out of his pocket.

I slumped in my chair and cast a doubtful look. "Splenda?"

"It's not 'Splenda'. It's melatonin."

I leaned over the table and whispered. "Drugs, Samuel? Really?"

He pulled back, shocked. "It's not a street drug. It's a hormone produced by the pineal gland in the brain. It's responsible for controlling circadian rhythms—the sleep and wake cycles. It's recommended by doctors to help people with jet lag."

"I'm confused. How is this supposed to help me 'surf my brain?' I'm not jet lagged."

"Aren't you? You're traveling out of your time zone, with varying degrees of ambient light fluctuation. It's not the same as traveling from North America to Europe, but the effects on your brain and physical body are quite similar."

Hmm. "I suppose that would explain why fatigue is such a big issue. Especially on return."

"Exactly." He held the packet over my cup of tea. "May I?"

I nodded.

"Melatonin comes in the form of little white pills, easily dissolvable, but I found it works more efficiently if you grind it up first."

I stirred in the white power and took a sip, preparing for some weird chemical taste, but it was surprisingly pleasant. I waited for Samuel to add some to his tea, but he didn't do it. I raised a brow in question.

"I've had enough experience and practice that I no longer need the assistance of melatonin," he explained.

We finished our tea and I waited for some big mind-altering experience, but nothing unusual happened.

"Now what?" I asked.

Samuel scooted his chair back. "Let's go outside."

I followed Samuel to the edge of the parking lot. He took my hand. "Now we relax." I loved how his old, leathery hand felt wrapped around mine.

"Right here?"

Samuel grinned. "There's nothing here in 1863. It's a perfect place to *chill out*, as you kids like to say."

It was weird hearing him talk to me like I was so much younger than him, because when we first met in 1863, we were the same age.

"Okay, I'm chillin'." I rolled my shoulders, closed my eyes, and took a long, deep breath while I visualized myself surfing all the way back to the Watsons.

A few moments later, Samuel's warm voice mumbled, "You ready?"

"Yes," I said without opening my eyes. I felt comfortable, but dizzy. I smiled as the white tunnel of light burned red through my eyelids.

I fought to keep my balance as I took in my altered surroundings and blinked back tears at the sight of the large farmhouse in the distance, nestled in poplar trees next to a sparkling pond. Linen blew in the wind on a clothesline in the back yard and children's voices floated on the breeze.

"I'm back," I whispered.

Samuel full lips broke into a bright-white smile. "You're back."

I grabbed at my heart and hopped on my tip-toes. "You can't imagine how happy I am right now!"

A woman with fiery red hair piled on the top of her head, came out of the back of the house and began to remove the laundry from the line. I mouthed, "Sara."

I turned to Samuel. "She'll marry Henry Abernathy and have six kids."

Samuel cocked a brow. "And how would you know this?"

I smiled slyly. "I have my ways."

"Well, I'm happy that you're happy, but my old legs are ready to go home. It's past my bedtime."

"Just like that? You can go back anytime you want?" I knew Samuel insinuated that, but I still found it hard to believe.

"You can watch me go."

I threw my arms around him and breathed in his Old-Spice-old-man smell. "Thanks so much for your help, Samuel."

"It was my pleasure. And I hope you get to where it is you want to go."

"Me, too."

"Good-bye, Casey." Samuel stepped away, closed his eyes, and clasped his hands together over his chest. He took several long breaths and I began to worry that his attempt to travel back to his realm would fail when his body began to shimmer. Then with a snap, he was gone.

"Bye, Samuel."

It was so weird to see him disappear like that. Was it that easy? Could I go home now, too? I closed my eyes and folded my arms across my chest. I took several deep cleansing breaths, willing myself into a state of relaxation. I

185

thought about home. About Mom and Dad and Tim. About Lucinda. Nate. My Nate, not an odd, alternate-reality version of Nate.

I did my best statue imitation, but nothing happened. After fifteen minutes, I gave up. Samuel said he had tested and experimented with his travel-control for a long time before he perfected it. Who was I to think I would see success on my first try?

I rubbed my palms on my jeans and took in my twenty-first century clothing. I knew my way to my stash from here: I just hoped I'd remembered to restock it. There was some new growth in the woods, but with a little trial and error I picked up my footpath, wading through the over grown branches. Every so often a twig would snag in my curls and I'd get tugged back with a yelp. Eventually I made it to the lilac grove that encircled my stash. It had a small opening in the centre, like the bald spot of a large, old man's head. A dry log lay beside the remnants of a small fire pit. I selected a sturdy stick and bent down to start digging under a rock I used as a marker.

It was a shallow hole, but big enough to house a jar of stale water, a plastic bag of dried fruit and a costume—a pale blue, floor-length, every-day dress women wore in the civil war era that I'd picked up at the costume shop in Cambridge.

I waved the dress to air it out, giving it a few good snaps in an effort to work out the wrinkles. It smelled like earth and there was no hope to extinguish the wrinkles without the help of an industrial-strength iron. Though I knew I was alone, instinct had me double-checking my privacy. Once assured, I removed my clothes and slipped into the dress. The great thing about long dresses, even with my height, was that I could conceal my shoes. Wearing flats helped. I just had to remember to keep my feet tucked under my chair while sitting. It was the proper posture for ladies in this era anyway, along with a straight back, and hands folded in the lap.

I had a hair tie stored on my wrist, so I used it to gather my curls and create an updo. It wasn't stylish, but it was off the neck, which was the important part. Wild, loose hair belonged to the hookers of this age, and I'd rather be deemed unfashionable and somewhat uncivilized than mistaken for that.

At this point I had no choice but to sip from the stale water. My throat was miserably dry, and I still had a good trek back to the farm ahead of me. I grimaced as I sipped. It was warm and tasted bad, but it was wet. I screwed the lid on and placed the jar back into the hole, along with my street clothes. I tossed a handful of raisins into my mouth before returning the bag of dried fruit. I brushed the area over with a broken sprig and replaced the rock.

I used the time walking back to the farm trying to come up with another story. This was the part I hated the most—lying to the Watsons about why I kept leaving and arriving at sporadic stretches of time. To their credit, they'd grown use to the way I dropped in and left without notice and no longer questioned me about it so much.

I heard male voices as I approached the main road, and automatically dropped low behind the brush and out of sight. Even though I was dressed for the era, I was a woman and alone, a situation that was frowned upon by common society, and was also potentially dangerous.

A small regiment of soldiers marched by. Dressed in worn gray trousers and blue Union jackets, they shuffled their old boots and walked with slumped shoulders. Each one had a musket propped over one shoulder and a bag filled with their belongings over the other. This despondent group was nothing like the soldiers I'd seen in the past—eager, zealous and certain of victory.

I held my breath and waited until they were out of sight, and after checking that no other foot traffic or horse and buggy traffic was in the distance, I continued on my way.

It'd been almost a year since I'd been back. A year in this time where war was the only thing on the minds and hearts of the people. Many folks in these parts had been notified by now of the death of a son and brother.

When the farm came into view, I paused to get my breath and to wipe away the sweat that had formed on my brow. I made my way to the back, to the door of the kitchen where family and the farm workers entered the house.

I knocked.

The door cracked open, and Sara's red head appeared. Her face broke out into a smile. "Cassandra! Aren't you a sight for sore eyes."

"Hi, Sara." I couldn't stop myself from pulling her into a hug. "It so good to see you!"

"It's been a long time. I was beginning to wonder if you'd ever come by again."

"I know," I agreed. "It's been too long, but I'm here now!"

I looked around the large kitchen. The long wooden table that had hosted many meals and lively conversation sat along one wall, opposite of a impressive wood stove and large porcelain sink (without running water).

With a family as large as the Watsons, it was strangely quiet.

"Where is everyone?" I asked.

"Duncan has joined Willie in the army. Father is in New York on business—the war has made everyone frantic and busy. There aren't any men left in Boston to hire for the farm, they've all been drafted, so the running of the farm is on my and my mother's shoulders."

Sara's happy greeting had temporarily erased the fatigue that now showed on her face in the form of dark under-eye circles. She let out a tired breath. "The other children except for baby Daniel who's napping upstairs and Ma are sowing seeds in the fields at the moment. I'm about to prepare a meal for when they return."

She smiled again. "They'll be so happy to see you."

"And I can't wait to see them. I bet they've all grown so much since I've seen them last."

"I can assure you, they have."

I pushed up the sleeves of my dress. "How can I help?"

"Would you like to slice the bread?"

"Sure."

The bread was homemade, of course, and heavier than usual. I had the feeling that rations on staples contributed to the necessity of using a simpler recipe. I didn't say anything or complain. I knew very little about the hardships they'd been under these last many months.

"Have you heard from Willie?" I asked.

"Sadly, no. I keep waiting for the post to arrive, but mail service seems slower than ever."

"What about from Henry?"

Sara's eyes darted to me and then back to the soup she was preparing. Her sudden shyness along with the flare of red in her cheeks spoke of her continued attachment to Henry Abernathy.

"No. Nothing from him in weeks."

"I'm sorry. It must be so hard to go so long without hearing anything." At least in my time, we had the Internet—communications were quick and often.

"It is." She wiped at a stray tear. "Sometimes I feel like I can no longer bear it. If it weren't for the children and my mother...I don't know if I could even get out of bed in the morning."

I wished I could offer her words of comfort. But I knew the outcome of this war and it wasn't good.

We had the soup and bread ready just as the Watson troop burst through the door. They were a dirty, weary version of the kids I remembered, but their smudged-up faces brightened when they saw me.

"Cassandra!" I gave them all big hugs, hoping my energy would revive them a little, including one to the petite and bone-thin matriarch.

"Hello, Mrs. Watson," I said.

Mrs. Watson always seemed fragile to me, but today her inner strength shone through. "Welcome, my dear. So nice to have a friendly face to brighten the day."

The toll the war was taking on this family was evident and I hated to see them so down. "It's nice to be here. I'm just passing through, but wanted to check in."

"You're always welcome here," she said with a fondness that made feel warm and sad at the same time.

Sara clapped her hands to gain the children's attention. "Go wash up. We don't want the soup to get cold."

The kids disappeared upstairs to the bowls and pitchers of water that would be found in each room. Soon after they returned with damp faces, some more clean than others.

I did my best to keep the conversation light around the table. "How's Nellie?" I asked. Nellie was the favorite family horse.

The oldest sister next to Sara, Josephine, answered. "She's good. We're down to two mares and a gelding, now."

Josephine brushed dark curls off her face, and asked softly, "How's Timothy? Is he still on the field?"

Josephine and Timothy had once shared a crush, back before Timothy brashly ran away with the army. I decided a form of the truth would work here. "He was injured, but is at home now, safe."

"Not seriously, I hope?"

"He'll walk with a limp the rest of his life, but at least he's alive."

"How about Nathaniel?" Sara asked. "Have you any word?"

Nate. I hadn't actually thought about him since my arrival. Which was odd, since he was a big part of my most dramatic memories here.

I shook my head. "No."

I announced that I'd do all the clean up. "Please allow me. I don't mind, really. Go get some rest."

"Your offer is so kind," Sara said. "We are all so terribly tired. But you also must be?"

"I've had a second wind since arriving. Don't worry about me."

"Okay. Thank you. You can sleep with Josephine and me," Sara said. "You know where my room is upstairs."

"Actually, if you don't mind, I'd like to stay in the cabin, if it's available."

Sara looked at me with a confused look in her eye. "It's available, but why would you want to sleep there, alone?"

"I'm used to being alone. And I need some time to think."

"Then you are welcome to it. The sheets inside are clean."

"Great. Goodnight then."

"See you in the morning, Cassandra."

I couldn't make any promises, but I nodded. Then I poured the water that had been heating up on the stove into the sink and started the dishes.

Chapter Twenty—Two

Dusk had fallen by the time I finished with the kitchen. I turned off all the oil lamps except the one I carried across the yard with me. Crickets chorused loudly along with pond frogs. I'd forgotten how loud it could get here at night, even without vehicle noise. I slapped at the mosquitoes that buzzed about my head.

The cabin was unlocked: in fact, it didn't have a lock, and I let myself in. I stood still in the light of the lantern and took it in. It was small, with a wood stove in one corner, a table under the window set with a bowl and pitcher and two cots against either wall. I smiled softly at the blanket that still hung between them, my attempt at privacy when I shared the space with my "brother" Nathaniel.

Our romance had begun here. Well not our romance, but our friendship, which eventually led to our romance.

I put the lamp on the table and poured the water into the bowl so I could wash my face. I didn't relish the idea of using the outhouse out back in the dark, but I thought sooner was better than later, so I grabbed the lamp and followed the path, awkwardly mussing with my skirts to get the job done.

Once back in the cabin, I washed my hands with the bar of handmade soap. It was mid-May and the evenings were chilly, so I started a small fire. I remembered all the times I watched Nate bending low to tend to this task. He was everywhere I looked. I lay on my cot and in my mind I could see Nate lying on his side, facing me, a cocky grin on his face. This was before I had the sheet hung, but I knew this had been a common posture for him.

I remembered all the awkward conversations, and how I had to explain about my time-travel life, how difficult it was for him to grasp, but how eventually he took on my wellbeing here as his responsibility.

For two years Nate had known about everything that went on with me when I traveled. He grew angry at the times I ended up coming back without him.

If he only knew the shenanigans I'd been up to lately.

Marlene's wild party and Lolly's arranged marriage in 1929. All the changed time-lines with versions of him that I, quite honestly, wished I didn't know. My adventures during the era of the War of Independence.

Samuel's surprising yet simple discovery.

It hurt my heart that Nate didn't know about these ventures, and that he apparently no longer cared.

I, however, still cared for him. I couldn't deny the aching in my heart. I felt broken, but strangely, no longer lost. I had a decision to make about my future, and as I drifted to sleep, I already knew what I was going to do.

The rooster worked just as consistently during war time as during peace and I groaned as its crowing pulled me out of slumber.

I went through what was once my normal routine here: used the outhouse, washed up, collected a water pail and went to the well where I manually pumped a lever to fill it, carried it carefully to the kitchen in an attempt to avoid having the water slosh out over the rim.

Sara was already up and making pancakes when I arrived.

"Good morning, Cassandra!" she said. "I hope you slept well."

I placed the heavy pail on the floor by the sink. "Extremely."

I fell into place like one of the family, setting the table and helping the younger children dress. Michael and Jonathon returned from milking the cows, a signal that it was time to eat. I loved how everyone gathered for meals, three times a day.

We were part way through breakfast when there was a tap on the door.

Josephine scooted out from the table. "I'll get it." She returned excitedly, waving two envelopes. "The post came! There's one from Henry and one from Willie!" She handed the letter from Henry to Sara. She tucked it under her arm. I didn't blame her for wanting to read Henry's letter in private. It could be full of romantic mush!

She motioned to Josephine. "Read Willie's to us."

Josephine used a knife to carefully break the seal. Her fingers trembled as she held the thin paper.

"Dear family,

I'm writing to you from Virginia. You'll be happy to know I'm still all in one piece, though that piece is shrinking by the day. The food here is deplorable! Ma and Sara, how I miss your cooking!

Sleeping can be tough, especially when your tent mate snores, and you have a secondary army waging nightly battles in the form of insects.

However, my regime remains in fine form. I have Henry and James to keep me company, though I do grow tired of Henry's inability to stop talking about one pretty redhead!"

Josephine paused to titter, and the younger kids laughed. Sara's complexion turned nearly as red as her hair.

Josephine inhaled deeply and continued,

"We march on to Chancellorville in the morn. Perhaps we'll continue to be beaten down by boredom, rather than actual battle.

I remember you all in my prayers each night, as I know you do me.

Until we meet again.

197

All my love,
Willie"

A small cheer went up in the room.

"My heart is refreshed," Mrs. Watson said, dabbling her eyes. "I am fortified to wait longer until he finally returns safe and sound."

"Josephine," I said. "What is the date of that letter?"

She glanced at the sheet in her hand. "The fifteenth of April. Nearly three weeks ago."

"And today's date? Sorry, I've lost track."

Sara answered. "It's the sixth of May."

I felt my lips quiver, and I turned away so they couldn't see. I was the only one in the room who knew that Willie had died two days ago.

Sara touched my sleeve. "Is everything okay?"

"Sara, I'm afraid I must leave. I beg of you to continue to be patient and understanding with me."

I raced outside and rounded the corner of the big house. I didn't have Samuel's skills of time-travel management. I was seriously out of control.

Chapter Twenty—Three

I d grown dizzy in the Watson kitchen and escaped just in time to fall through a blast of light.

I now stood in the parking lot in front of the tea shop at the strip mall in Somerville. I wore my jeans, my red blouse and tan jacket. The wind whipped my hair and I pulled it off my face. I was back, but to which timeline? Was this the one with the Samuel who helped me get back to 1863, or was this *mine?*

One thing I'd learned was that everything could look the same, and not be the same.

Except if this was the Samuel-who-helped-me timeline, then he would be standing in this parking lot with me, right? Since I always returned to the exact spot I'd left. At least that was the way it worked before I broke the laws.

199

My heart surged with hope.

I had enough change in my pocket to catch the train back to Cambridge. I couldn't stop myself from leaning my head back and closing my eyes. I thought about Willie Watson. His reddish-brown curls, his big smile. How we first met as pre-pubescent kids and I'd fooled him into thinking I was a boy.

I loved him like a brother.

Up until now, there had always been a chance we'd see each other when I tripped back to their time. But now... now he really was dead, in my time and his. A large lump formed in my throat and I rubbed my neck as I struggled to swallow.

My stop approached as I worked to pull myself together. The walk home felt longer than it actually was, and my legs moved like they were made of rubber. All I wanted to do was hop into bed and sleep.

Please let this be my home!

I turned into my drive and froze. I'd expected Tim's car and even hoped to see Tim in the yard, the kind-hearted version who walked with a limp, but I didn't expect an old model BMW. I didn't expect Nate.

He was sitting on my front steps and stood when he saw me, thrusting fists into his front jeans pockets the way he always did when he was nervous.

"Hey," he said.

"Hey." I wasn't absolutely sure this was *my* Nate. "What are you doing here?"

"I wanted to see you." He walked toward me until we were a couple feet apart. He squinted as he studied my eyes. "You just tripped."

He knew. None of the other Nates knew about my time-tripping life. My lips tugged up. I was home.

"I did."

"Where? I mean when?"

"Does it matter?" I heard the bitterness creep into my voice. "I thought you didn't want to concern yourself with my life anymore. I'm resourceful and capable, remember?"

The thing was, he was right. I *was* resourceful and capable. I had handled everything that was thrown at me over the last few days and weeks all on my own.

"Casey," Nate said softly. "I'm sorry."

I sighed. "Me too. That was harsh. You have every right. And obviously, I'm fine. I *am* okay on my own."

"I don't want you to be on your own. I'm not just here to apologize, but to tell you I love you. I over-reacted about that…thing with King. For better or worse, we're meant to be together."

This was the moment in the movies where the couple, thwarted in every way, finally come together for their happily ever after. I should've been overjoyed.

Why wasn't I?

Even though this Nate hadn't been spending time with me, I'd been spending time with versions of him. Versions that proved that under other circumstances, we weren't necessarily meant for each other.

I sighed, feeling tired and confused.

201

Nate's expression grew desperate. "Say something."

"I don't know what to say, Nate. It's true, I'm fine, but I've been through a lot. I need some time."

He held his palms up. "Sure. You can have all the time you need. I'm here when you're ready. Please, just call me, okay?"

I stepped away, toward my front door. "Okay."

Inside my house, I closed the door and leaned against it heavily. All along I had been looking for a way to make things right with Nate, hoping for an opportunity like the one he'd just offered me—and now that it had come, I didn't take it.

I definitely needed to sleep.

I took a cursory look around. Everything appeared to be in order. Dad's things, mom's things, Tim's things.

My things. All were where they should be. I found Mom bent over her desk in her office upstairs.

"Hi, Mom."

She lowered her glasses. "Hi Casey. Nate was here looking for you."

"I saw him outside."

She sat up straight and squinted at me. "Is everything okay between you?"

"Yeah. I'm just gonna have a nap."

"The last days leading up to grad are exhausting, I know," she said as I walked out. "I'll call you for dinner."

I slept through until five in the morning. Mom was used to my occasional sleep binges, attributing them to my demanding studies and general teenage stuff she had given up trying to wake me to eat.

I quietly made my way to the kitchen, so grateful for the espresso machine that quickly made me one cup of excellent coffee. Back in my room, I opened my laptop. I had a little time to burn before I needed to get ready for school. I searched for college applications.

An hour later, Tim poked his head into my room. He rubbed sleep from his eye. "You okay?"

I wanted to spring up and give him a thanks-for-being-alive-and-not-a-jerk hug, but didn't want to freak him out. "Yeah, just catching up on homework."

"I wanna hear about it later."

I played coy. "Hear about what?"

"Ha. You don't fool me. I know you tripped. I want the deets."

I wasn't sure he'd be to pleased with these particular "deets." I shrugged casually.

He went on, "I have an early study class this morning so unless you want to get there early, you'll have to bum a ride with Lucinda."

"I'll text her, thanks."

He limped down the hall and into the bathroom. Moments later the shower began.

Lucinda was fine about picking me up, but the clock was ticking and I needed to get ready, otherwise she'd be honking and we'd be chasing down late slips. Fortunately, I wasn't the type who needed a lot of time.

I found clean jeans and a cute long-sleeve T, and threw them on. I tied my curls back and applied mascara, then I chose brown faux leather flat-heeled boots and added a long-knit sweater.

Mom and Dad were finishing breakfast when I entered the kitchen. It was so good to see them together and normal—my own real life. I couldn't stop grinning at them.

"Sleep put you in a good mood," Mom said.

Dad appraised me with admiration in his eye. "She looks ready to take on the world."

Mom pushed a plate of toast my way. "There's a couple left. Help yourself."

I smothered them with peanut butter and jelly, and nearly inhaled them. I was famished.

I brushed crumbs off my face and put my dirty dishes in the dishwasher—I loved dishwashers!

Lucinda honked just as I was finished brushing my teeth and applying lip gloss. I skipped out the door, so happy to see her.

"Hey, girl," Lucinda said cheerily as I got in. "Sleep much?"

I snapped on my seatbelt. "What? I was up early."

Lucinda looked over her shoulder as she backed out of my drive. "Have you checked your missed calls? I was starting to get worried, so I called your mom. She said you'd been in bed since you got home from school."

"I'm a growing girl."

"You're a *busy* girl, and I want to hear all about it."

First Tim, now Lucinda. I guess I couldn't blame them for being curious. Plus the fact that she was even asking was just further proof that she was *my* Lucinda and that I was back.

"Chop, chop," Lucinda said. "We've got twenty minutes until we get to school."

"I don't even know where to start."

"Last I heard you were tripping to 1929 and had returned to an alternate timeline, which," she waved a hand, "you obviously fixed."

"I've actually been to a few altered timelines."

Lucinda cocked a nicely shaped brow. "What was I like? I hope we were still friends."

"We were friends, but…"

"But?"

"Well, in one of them, you were with Nate."

"What! Shut the door! I'd never do that to you, Casey. Wait. Are you still broken up?"

"You didn't do anything to me Lucinda, because in that timeline, Nate and I were never together."

"Oh, God. You must be so messed up."

I made a raspberry sound with my lips. "I am, kind of."

I gave her the Sparks Notes version of the rest of my travels, including my time with the Reveres and how Samuel helped me reset my loop. And how Nate had come to see me yesterday.

We'd been sitting in her car in the school parking lot for at least ten minutes, Lucinda's mouth hanging wide open.

"So, what about Nate, then? Are you together again?"

"I told him I needed time. You can see why, can't you?"

"Oh, yeah."

The second bell went and we had to sprint to make it to our first class.

If I wanted to graduate with decent marks, I had to put my problems away and focus on my classes. I was glad that Nate wasn't in school with me anymore and that I didn't have any relational distractions.

Austin King gave me a chin nod, but I kept my eyes lowered. If he only knew that in a version of this reality we were actually together…oh, man. I blushed with embarrassment. Even though he had no recollection of kissing me beyond that one fateful kiss, I had clear memories of kissing him. Truth was, he was a good kisser and except for how it messed with my heartstrings, I didn't mind it much at all.

Lucinda sat with Sam Capone in the cafeteria at lunch. He had a well-build arm draped over her slender back. Her sleek dark hair was swooped over one shoulder and she gazed up at him like he was the only guy in the room.

She sat up straight when she spotted me, and waved me over. "Here, I bought you lunch today."

There was an extra tray with an egg salad sandwich on whole grain bread, a cherry yogurt and a chocolate milk.

"Thanks, Mom," I said, taking the seat beside her

Sam looked over Lucinda's head and flashed me a half-grin in greeting. "What's up?"

I peeled the plastic off my sandwich. "Not much."

Lucinda snorted. "Understatement of the year." She leaned in closer and whispered. "Don't think you're done talking. I know you skipped stuff."

My mouth was full so I just muffled agreement. Lucinda was like a dog with a bone when she wanted something and wouldn't give up questioning me until she knew *everything*.

The loud din of cafeteria chatter suddenly went silent. Heads turned toward the caf entrance. I spun around just as three police officers walked to our table.

My mind scrambled for a reason—had I done something? Maybe I'd created a time riff I wasn't aware of and was going to get thrown into jail. *Again.*

But it wasn't me they were after.

"Sam Capone, you're under arrest for running an illegal online gambling ring that targets minors."

Oh, no. What I feared about Sam Capone was true?

Gasps of disbelief and tabloid-worth chatter crescendoed in the room. Sam was eighteen and could be tried as an adult now. He groaned and pushed away from the table. One of the cops slapped handcuffs on his hands.

I cast a worried glance at Lucinda. She burst into tears.

Chapter Twenty—Four

Two weeks later was the night of the prom and both Lucinda and I were without dates.

She'd cried for two days before shaking off Sam Capone like dust on her feet. "He's so not worth it," she'd said. "It's just a bummer not to have a date for the prom."

I'd agreed. "We don't even need to go to at all."

"Of course we're going!" Lucinda said. "You said yourself that you don't need a guy to go to the dance."

Now we stood in my bedroom, wearing the dresses we'd bought before my class trip to Hollywood when we had shared a rosy and romantic ideal of what our prom would be like.

My gown was mid-length and shimmery teal, and Lucinda's was a deep purple.

We'd helped each other with our up-dos and commented on make-up choices.

Lucinda appraised me. "You look great, Casey."

"Thank you. So do you."

We spritzed each other with perfume and added earrings and other finishing touches. Mine included a pair of long lace gloves. I gingerly put them on, pausing a moment to rub the small scar on my forearm.

"No slow dancing for me," I said. Even with the gloves, a guy might touch my bare shoulders. I couldn't risk taking anyone back accidentally again.

"Me, either, duh," Lucinda said. "Only group dancing to fast songs!"

"Exactly!"

Mom took pictures as Tim and Dad looked on.

Mom gushed. "You girls are so beautiful! Come on, smile!"

Tim placed a thumb to his nose and wiggled his fingers, making me laugh. I glowed and felt grateful for my family and for my BFF who'd stuck with me through thick and thin.

"Okay," Lucinda said. "I promised my mom and sisters we'd stop in for pictures too, so if we want to get to the prom before the last dance is announced, we gotta go."

It was only a slight exaggeration. We suffered through a lot of flashes and a deluge of Portuguese from them, but finally we were free of family and at the actual dance. Our tickets had been prepaid, so we only had to produce ID to get our hands stamped and let inside.

The hall was beautifully decorated with flowers and spinning lights. A refreshment table was located along the far wall and a DJ was busy at the end of the darkened room. Dance music played loudly and the crowd of grads jumped in time with the beat.

"Come on, Casey!" Lucinda dragged me by the elbow onto the dance floor and we joined in. I laughed. We'd come without dates, and no one cared. Everyone kind of danced with each other. Just one big group having fun.

We had to come up for air after the fourth song. I shouted over the music, "I need a drink!"

Lucinda nodded and followed me to the refreshment table. I grabbed an extra napkin to delicately mop my face, before accepting a drink from the server.

All the free chairs were taken, so we moved to the wall and leaned against the cool bricks. I closed my eyes and breathed deeply, feeling happy.

Lucinda nudged me with her elbow. "Nate."

"I already told you, Lucinda. I'm fine alone."

"No, it's Nate!"

What?

My eyes snapped open and I followed Lucinda's gaze. Little sparks of nerves lit up through my body. It was déjà vu. Just like the Fall Dance back in our sophomore year, Nate Mackenzie walked toward me, shimmering in the lights like a mirage. He wore a dark blue tux, a crisp white shirt and a black tie.

He looked amazing.

I choked out, "Am I hallucinating?"

Lucinda cocked her head. "If you are, then I am, too."

Nate approached and stood with his hands behind his back. "Good evening, ladies."

"What are you doing here?" It sounded rude, but I was just in shock.

"If you recall, Casey, I had a ticket."

Right. Prepaid. Nate was my "plus one".

"I'm going…" Lucinda began, "to go…over there." She headed for the ladies room, leaving me alone. I swallowed and met Nate's gaze.

He held out an arm. "Would you like to dance?"

I smiled as I accepted it. "Certainly."

As fate would have it, the DJ chose this moment to slow things down. Nate held my hand in the air, while placing the other around my waist. I held on to his shoulder.

Nate whispered in my ear, sending shivers down my spine. "You look beautiful."

"You look pretty good yourself," I said.

"You made it, Casey. Graduation's around the corner. Then college."

I understood his implication. Then we'd be together attending Boston University as planned.

I pulled back to look into his deep-blue eyes. "I've applied to NYU."

Nate blinked. "You're not changing your plans to come to BU because of me, are you? Because of what I said, because, I'm sorry. You know that, right?"

"I know, Nate. It's not because of you. It's what I actually want. I chose BU because I didn't think I had a real choice. I thought I had to stay in Boston. And yes, I wanted to be with you."

He frowned. "And now you don't?"

"I didn't say that."

He pulled me closer and we circled around in silence. I knew it was Nate's way of processing things.

I spoke into his ear. "Is that why you went to BU? Because of me? Are you sorry you didn't go to York?"

"I'm not sorry I didn't go to York. I wanted to go to BU. Having you join me was a major bonus. I'll admit to being disappointed that you're changing your plans."

"I don't mean to hurt you. I think I've always wanted to go to NYU, but I was afraid to leave Boston because of... my condition. One thing I've learned recently is that I can deal with new people and places. Even times. I know I'll find my way, wherever I go."

Nate pulled me closer. "I'm sorry I had to lose you for you to find that out."

I didn't know what to say to that. I let my head rest on his shoulder. "I'm going to miss you. A lot."

"I'll miss you, too."

I licked off a salty tear that ran down my cheek and onto my lip.

"I'm sorry that it turned out like this," I said. "That I kissed Austin."

"Shh. It's okay. I hope you'll get a chance to kiss a lot of different guys in New York."

I pulled back to study his expression. "Do you really?"

"Well, no." Sadness crossed his face. "That's a lie. I don't want any guy besides me to ever touch you again." He sighed and swirled me around. "In fact, I may have come to New York to punch out a few lights."

"Would you come to New York?" I asked. "Not to punch guys, but to visit me?"

Nate slowed us to a stop. "Do you mean it?"

I nodded. "Yes. But as friends."

Nate's expression dropped. "Friends?"

I answered firmly. "Friends."

Chapter Twenty—Five

Three Months Later

To the surprise of my parents and especially my brother and Lucinda, I applied and was accepted into New York University's Creative Writing Program. Even after three weeks, I could barely believe I was here. I sat in theater-style seating, mid-way up, near the aisle. The American Literature class was a popular one, full, with the exception of a few empty chairs. The prof, a middle-age woman with short hair tucked behind her ears and black-framed glasses, read a passage from Hemingway. The energy in the room was ripe with the eagerness of college freshmen, excited to be away from home for the first time.

I had been a little intimidated the first few days

after arriving in New York City, with its noise and frenetic pulse. So different from Boston. Boston was like an old professor who had been wild in his youth, but had tempered with age and was comfortable now, wearing a cardigan and smoking a pipe. New York was like a rocker who got older but hadn't grown up, still wearing unbuttoned shirts and turning the amplifier up to ten.

But I got why people loved it. It pulsed with life! The people were ambitious and full of hope. They came to pursue their artistic dreams, like I had, or had come from far away places to follow the American dream. It was a hive of hurried, busy, driven people living under neon lights and clusters of dramatic billboards. Pedestrians of every nationality and with varied fashion sensibilities scurried about night and day, always a deadline or an adventure to pursue. It was true that NYC was a city that never slept.

I'd been riding public transit all my life so it hadn't taken me too long to figure out how to navigate between my campus and the student housing where I shared a tiny, furnished apartment with a blond, full-figured girl named Chelsea who was also in the arts program.

I still thought about Nate. A lot. He took my decision to revert to "friends" seriously (meaning that we weren't friends at all), and pretty much kept his distance from me all summer. Except for that one time we met up at the park by my house. I didn't know why I had agreed to meet him there. We sat on the very bench we had sat on the day we first officially became a couple, the day I had mistakenly thought Nate was going to give me the let's-just-be-friends-speech and instead gave me the surprising I-want-to-be-more-than-friends speech.

We had come full circle and it killed me. There had been a good two feet on the bench between us and Nate's expression was dour.

"Before you leave for NYU," he'd said, "can you tell me what happened? Did you stay in 1929? With Marlene?"

His blue eyes pleaded with mine and I knew he wouldn't rest, wouldn't be able to *let go*, until he understood everything. I decided to tell him the whole truth. That it was Lolly Kavanaugh, a girl he hadn't met, who turned out to be my friend in 1929, and not Marlene Charter as he had predicted. About my surprise entanglement with Paul Revere Junior that took me back to 1775. Shock washed over his face at that revelation, but to his credit, he didn't interrupt me.

I told him about all the different versions of him I'd encountered and our altered relationships.

When he finally spoke, he said softly, "I can't believe I'd ever want anyone but you."

I stared back, unblinking. "But you did."

A pained expression crossed his face as he nodded subtly with comprehension. I felt mine tighten with sadness. This was the end.

We hugged each other as we said goodbye and I choked back sobs as I speed-walked back to my house, arms wrapped tightly around my chest as if my heart would burst out onto the sidewalk with a grotesque splat if I didn't hold it in.

If things had gone as originally planned, I'd be there attending BU with him.

I shook my head. Coming to NYU was the right decision for me. I had to move on from Nate Mackenzie.

The prof wrapped things up, and I realized with a shock that my mind had drifted and I'd blanked out on whatever she'd said in the last five minutes. Hopefully it wasn't important. Bodies shuffled past me and I stood to get out of the way, juggling my books and laptop. I followed the flow out of the room.

"Hey," a male voice said. A cute guy with a buzz cut and a crooked smile held up a book. "I think you dropped this."

Right. My copy of *To Kill a Mockingbird* was missing from my pile. "Oh." I reached for it. "Thanks."

"What'd you think?"

I was confused by his question. "Of what?"

"The book."

"Oh. It's great," I said lamely. "A classic for a reason."

"Can you imagine writing just *one* book, and it becoming a classic in your own lifetime?"

I shook my head. "No. I doubt Harper Lee could've imagined it, either."

There was a glint in his hazel eyes I recognized as interest. "I'm Brendan," he said. "From Minnesota."

I smiled in return. "Casey. From Massachusetts."

He nodded to my short stack of paperbacks. "Old school, huh?" He tapped on his tablet. "All my books are neatly kept in one spot."

"Yeah, I still like to read the old-fashioned way."

He tilted his head, his grin pulling up higher. "I've been known to open up an actual print book on occasion."

"Glad to see your biases are pliable."

He chuckled, then surprised me by saying, "Casey from Massachusetts, would you like to go out with me sometime?"

I felt my eyelids flutter. Would I like to go out with him? My heart skittered about my ribcage. Nate had told me to go out with new guys. Find out what it was that I was apparently missing by only ever having had one boyfriend. I felt unsteady, as if I were somehow about to walk the plank. Could I really have a life that didn't include Nate? I'd have to venture out over high seas to find out.

"I think I would, Brendan from Minnesota."

He nodded, pleased, and handed me his phone. I entered my number.

Brendan pushed the phone back into his pocket. "I'll call you."

He disappeared into the crowd. I stood there stunned at what had just happened.

I headed out of the building onto the busy sidewalk, my head spinning. Was I really going to go out with someone, *officially*, who wasn't Nate?

My admission just made the ending between us feel so real. So final.

I felt light-headed and for a moment, a little panicked. I clutched my backpack and grabbed at my heart. I hadn't tripped since the prom and not since arriving to New York. With all my brave talk about how I could handle *all the new things*, I still trembled at the thought of what might await me in nineteenth century New York City.

I waited for the burst of light and the free fall sensation, but it didn't happen. I let out a short breath of relief. Maybe I was growing out of random tripping. Wouldn't that be nice? All the thrusting about through time was hard on a body, not to mention my mental state. I envied Samuel. Inspired by his ability to control when he tripped, I had made several attempts to will myself back to the Watsons over the summer, but to no avail.

I hadn't made any efforts to test it out since arriving to New York, a situation I was now determined to change.

A week passed before I got a message from Brendan. Honestly, I thought he'd had a change of heart and I'd already put him out of my mind. My days were full of classes and studying and late night chats with my roomie.

Chelsea's blond eyebrows arched when I told her about Brendan. "Are you going to go?" she asked.

"I don't know. He waited a whole week before texting." Not even an actual phone call—just a text.

"So? The fact is he did text! He's interested! Do you have a picture?"

I pulled up his Facebook profile and spun my laptop around for her to see.

"Cute," she said, "in an army brat kind of way.

You definitely should go out with him."

I hummed. If my goal was to date other guys, here was my chance. It wasn't like there was a line up.

"Okay, I'll go," I said. "But I'm waiting until tomorrow to let him know."

"Playing hardball, huh?" Chelsea raised her hand to high five me and I slapped her palm. She blurted, "You go, girl!"

Our apartment was on the ground level of an old tenement building ten minutes away from the campus by bus. I shared the single bedroom with Chelsea, who'd claimed the top bunk. That was fine by me. I preferred the lower bunk. The view out our window was of the brick wall of the neighboring building less than eight feet away. The apartment overall was dark and smelled mildly of mold. I fished through my clothes wondering what I should wear to the movies—Brendan's choice for our first date—not that anyone would be looking in a darkened theatre. But there was the going in and coming out that mattered. I had to put in more effort than I would if I were going with Tim.

I dug through my limited wardrobe, then leaned against the bunk as I considered my options. I picked at the paint chipping off the wooden frame, noticing the different layers of color. The latest application was black, under that red, then white, then my nail scratched against the raw wood.

I wondered at my lack of enthusiasm. I should be more excited to be going out on a date with a cute boy.

I was just tired, that was all. I'd get my second

wind when I met up with him at the theatre. I selected a striped, long-sleeved T-shirt and a pair of jeans.

An hour and a half later I stood outside the theatre and scanned the crowds for a familiar face. I checked Brendan's message with the time and the address, confirming I was at the right place at the right time.

Finally, I spotted his shaved head and sauntering gait. He was ten minutes late but at least he hadn't stood me up. That would've been embarrassing and a real blow to my ego.

"Hey, Casey!" Brendan shouted. His gazed scanned me from head to toe and he his grin widened. "You look good."

"Thanks," I said. "So do you."

He laughed. "You're so cool. Most girls would go on about how they don't look good, fishing for extra compliments." He grabbed my hand and lead me to the ticket counter. His hand was warm and firm. Different from Nate's: smaller, but nice.

"I'll get it this time," he said as he pulled bills out of his pocket. I guess he assumed there would be a next time. And that I would pay. Which was fine. Equal rights and all that.

Nate would never let me pay.

Not because he didn't believe in equal rights, but because he still believed in chivalry.

Stop thinking about Nate!

"I can get the popcorn," I offered. Brendan shrugged. "Cool."

We made awkward conversation as we stood in the

concession line. *What's new? How are you? Did you finish your assignment?* Banal stuff like that. We made our way through the darkened theatre, and took seats in the middle section.

Brendan's movie choice was the latest Hollywood thriller. It was mindless but fun. The surround sound explosions thundered through the space. The action and adventure, including the mandatory car chase—in this case, motorbike chase—were enough to keep my mind from floating to the *boy-at-BU*.

About halfway through the movie, Brendan stretched out his arms and relaxed again as he lowered one arm around my shoulder. Smooth.

At first I stiffened, unsure about this next small step toward a new relationship. I hardly knew this guy. But wasn't that the reason we were hanging out? To get to know each other? I glanced at his hand that rested on my shoulder. I took a deep breath and forced myself to relax.

I kept my eyes glued to the big screen, nervous that if I glanced at him at all he'd take it as a sign I wanted to make out or something.

I didn't.

Finally, the credits rolled and the houselights were turned on.

"Incredible!" Brendan said.

"Yeah," I said to be polite, as nothing remarkable stuck out to me. "It was entertaining."

"That was a 2015 KTM 450 SXF! It has a 449 4-stroke engine with speeds up to 123 miles per hour. Man, I miss my bike!"

Brendan walked me home, threading his fingers

through mine with one hand and gesturing excitedly with the other.

"I have a 2001 Honda XR250R at home."

I widened my eyes and nodded, hoping I looked interested.

"I call her Hally, short for jalapeños, because she's red hot!"

I wondered if he realized that jalapeños was spelled with a J.

"You sound like you miss Minnesota," I said. "Why did you come to New York?"

He shrugged. "I wanted to see something different. Go on an adventure. You know what they say, 'you don't know what you have until it's gone?'"

Like Nate?

We made it to the front door of my building. Brendan put a hand up on the door jamb over my head and leaned closer. In a sultry voice he asked, "Can I come in?"

My stomach swirled. This guy moved too slow and then too fast!

"My roommate's home."

"Oh." Brendan's face flickered with disappointment, then he quickly recovered. "Okay. Well, I had fun tonight."

"Me, too."

He was too short to tilt his head down to mine, so he grabbed the back of my head with his hand and pulled my face to his. I closed my eyes and received the kiss.

Brendan's lips were thin, but soft. His tongue a

little too rapid. The kiss a little too wet. I moved back after an appropriate amount of time and glanced to the ground, surreptitiously wiping my mouth with my sleeve. I put on a smile when I looked back at him.

His lips tugged up in a satisfied grin. "Goodnight, Casey."

"Goodnight, Brendan."

He stepped away backward and held his thumb and pinky up to his ear. "I'll call you."

I nodded. "Okay."

I stepped inside the dim hallway of my building, waving to Brendan as I shut the door.

I'd gone on a date with someone who wasn't Nate.

I'd kissed another guy. That made three with Nate and Austin. I wasn't sure what number I was shooting for.

Brendan was going to call me. Which meant a second date, which might lead to a third and beyond.

Soon I could have a new boyfriend.

I should be ecstatic.

I felt sick.

I leaned my back against the door and slid slowly to the floor until I was resting on my heels. I was thankful the hallway was empty because I suddenly burst into tears. Then I fell into the light.

Chapter Twenty—Six

My structural support disappeared and I fell over onto my back with a groan. I quickly scrambled back to my feet, my eyes darting to take in my surroundings. No high-rises or automobiles. Horses and buggies on dusty streets.

New York City in 1863 was much like Boston, only bigger and busier. I dashed to escape being trampled by a horse and buggy, and tucked myself next to the outer wall of the nearest building. I worked to catch my breath. The rough bricks I leaned against dug into my shoulders. There were surprisingly few women about, only a few in the midst of crowds of men in dark trousers and jackets. Perhaps they were intimidated by the presence of the Union Army, or maybe they were too busy having to manage a home with fewer men about to help.

None of the women in the street wore pants. They had on dresses with ankle-length poofy skirts and tight

225

bodices. Long hair was braided or twisted up in a pile on their heads and covered with a bonnet or a frilly hat, depending on what social class the woman was from.

I slipped off the black hair band I regularly wore on my wrist and pulled my hair into a low ponytail, then tucked it into the back of my sweater in an effort to pass as a guy. Height gave me some leverage, but my curves were a problem. I hadn't come prepared. The best I could do was to untuck my shirt and slouch my shoulders.

I wasn't sure where to go or what to do. I didn't have my backpack that I'd carried with me 90% of the time, which contained shoes and a dress suitable for this era. I stayed tucked into the shadows as I sussed out my situation. Horses clopped by on the cobblestone streets pulling carts that carried commerce and the odd passenger. Men's voices rose above the din, their English accented heavily, mostly Irish or German. Occasionally a group of soldiers marched by.

Suddenly, there was a commotion to my left. A pretty young woman with dark hair poking out of her bonnet grasped at a younger girl in front of her. "Help!" she cried out. "My sister can't breathe! She's choking!"

A small crowd formed, and someone yelled out for a doctor, but no one came forward to help.

I sprung to the sisters without thinking of the consequence, grabbing the younger one. I wrapped my arms around her from behind, formed a fist and made short quick thrusts under her rib cage. Something dislodged and the younger girl spat the object to the ground. She breathed in deeply, color returning to the grayness of her cheeks, and burst out crying.

The crowd made grunts of appreciation. Noting the crisis had been averted, they gradually dispersed.

The young lady pulled her little sister to her chest, but her eyes stayed on me.

"We owe you a great debt, kind sir," she said with a lyrical accent, possibly Italian. "I don't know what you did, but, thank you."

I shrugged a shoulder and muttered with a lowered voice. "Just the Heimlich maneuver."

"Pardon?"

Belatedly I remembered that the Heimlich maneuver hadn't come into vogue until the 1970s. "Uh, nothing. Glad to help."

The woman held out her hand, "I am Marietta Ricci, and this is Donelle."

I was right about her being Italian. I shook her extended hand. "Casey Donovan."

It was handy to have a name that could be both a girl's or a guy's.

Marietta surprised me by linking her arm with mine. She held the smaller girl with her other hand and began walking. I worked on my "manly" gait, pointing my knees outward, keeping my hips stiff. It'd been a while since I had to pretend to be a guy and I was out of practice.

Marietta shot me a sideways glance and her smile turned down. I turned my face away from her, so she couldn't examine my chin too closely and the obvious lack of facial hair. My gaze landed on curious passersby. I quickly averted my eyes and tucked my chin lower. Man, I wished I had a hat!

Marietta spoke softly into my ear. "If you were a man posing as a girl, I would conclude you were dodging the draft. However, to be a girl and posing as a boy honestly has me baffled."

Busted.

"I can explain," I said, grateful to let my voice fall into its normal range.

"I'm eager to hear it," Marietta said.

I gently pulled my arm free from hers, my mind scrambling for the explanation I promised.

"I'm sorry," I finally said. "I can't say. I am in a bind, obviously, and if you could help me find a place to stay, out of sight, that would be appreciated."

Marietta gave me a sideways glance.

"Like a barn or something," I offered.

"Don't be ridiculous. You're coming home with us."

I dug my fists deeply into the front pocket of my jeans, continued slouching, eyes to the ground, praying to stay invisible. We passed a few wealthy men with gold watches leaking their chains from suit pockets, but mostly we strolled by middle class men in dusty outfits and some obviously poorer men with dirty faces, wearing colorless rags. Thankfully they paid little attention to me.

Marietta led us across a busy road, dodging horses and their riders, and turned down an intersecting street. Narrow three-story brick buildings pressed so closely together they looked like one long building lined the blocks. We stopped in front of one that had a black awning over a bay window on the ground floor that read in bold white lettering *Ricci's Produce*.

I followed Marietta inside. The walls were painted white but the floor and ceiling were covered in dark wood. A large "antique" register sat on the end of a counter, the tall kind with big round number keys for tallying the totals. Beside it was a copper scale for weighing the produce. Another girl with dark eyes and hair stood behind the counter, her gaze locked on me.

"Sabrina," Marietta began, "this is Casey. She's our guest."

Before Sabrina could question her sister about me, the bell over the door rang and a customer entered. Marietta nodded to Sabrina, then ushered me to the back of the room and up a set of narrow winding steps.

"The office and storage rooms are on the second floor," she said as we continued up the steps, "along with Papa's room. He works hard to keep us all clothed and fed. We do what we can to help, including things that men normally do. Like banking."

She opened the door to her bedroom. It was small, but tidy. Two single beds covered in handmade quilts sat on opposite sides of the room. Between them was a wooden chest of drawers topped with a hair brush and other sundry items, including an oil lamp. Marietta struck a match to light it.

"That's where I was. At the bank." She huffed. "Mr. Wright gladly takes our money, but doesn't want to give us any. 'War times are tough' he said. Like I didn't already know that. Why else would we need a loan?"

She snorted with contempt. "He was the one who

gave Donelle the candy, as if that would ease our troubles."

Marietta removed her bonnet and shawl and hung them on hooks that were fastened to the wall.

"Sabrina and Donelle are in the room across the hall. Leola and I are here. Lola can share a bed with Donelle for as long as needed." A flash of concern crossed her face. "She should be home by now."

A wooden wardrobe stood against the wall. Marietta eased past me and opened the doors. "Let's see what we can find for you to wear."

I peered out the window at the busy street below, then turned back to Marietta. She held a plain dress in the air and scrutinized it.

I wondered why there was no mention of a mama. Sometimes it was just best to ask. "What happened to your mother?"

Marietta answered without emotion. "She passed when Donelle was born." She walked the few steps it took to get to the window and held up a plain, brown dress. "I think this will fit."

I accepted the dress but didn't move. I was hoping I wouldn't be here long enough to have to put it on.

Marietta raised a dark brow. "You do know how to wear a dress, don't you? Or have you always pretended to be a boy?"

"I know how to wear a dress. I'll put it on in the morning."

She sighed. "It is getting late. No need to rush things, I suppose." She leaned on the sill and stared outside. "Now where is Leola?"

Then she gasped. "No. I forbade her!"

I followed her gaze until I spotted a dark-haired girl that resembled Marietta down the block on the corner. She stood face to face with a boy who held both of her hands in his.

This time it was my turn to gasp. From this distance, he looked like Nate!

Chapter Twenty—Seven

It didn t matter what I did or where I went, I couldn't escape Nate! My hand flew to my chest to settle my heart. Of course it *wasn't* him. How could it be? I hated how even a facsimile of Nate Mackenzie threw my pulse off course.

"She's gone and fallen for a *Protestant* German boy," Marietta explained. "I warned her to stay away from him. Oh, Lord. Papa's going to kill her if he finds out."

She picked up her skirts and hurried downstairs. I didn't know what else to do, so I followed her.

Marietta paused briefly to glance in the office on the second floor, the door was ajar enough to make out the bulky form of a man sitting behind a desk—"Papa," I assumed—then continued down to the main shop entrance where a young girl resembling Marietta stepped inside.

"Leola!"

Leola startled at the sudden approach of her sister, but then calmly removed her bonnet and shawl. "What are you so frantic about?"

"You know darn well what. I saw you out the window!"

Leola shrugged, seemingly indifferent. "I'm back in time to make the evening meal, aren't I? Just leave me be."

"What if Papa saw you?"

"He didn't, did he? Now if you'd just shush up!" Leola brushed past her sister defiantly and disappeared into a room I could only assume was the kitchen.

Trip fatigue was hitting me hard. I was more tired than hungry, having recently stuffed myself with popcorn at the theatre with Brendan. I wondered how he would handle it if I ever accidentally brought him back.

"Marietta, would you mind terribly if I skipped supper? I'll join you for breakfast and I'd be happy to do whatever chore you have for me tomorrow."

"You owe us no service," she said. "It is we who are in your debt. Please, make yourself at home."

"Thank you." I left Marietta to manage her sisters and dragged myself back up the steps.

Instead of undressing and crawling under the covers like I normally would, I lay flat on my back on Leola's bed, hands folded over my stomach.

Samuel said he'd learned to control his trips by

233

relaxing and concentrating. I felt sleepy enough. I just needed to relax and concentrate on tripping back home. I didn't know why I hadn't tried this before. I had just assumed tripping was something I'd never be able to control.

I focused on my present life in New York City. My apartment with Chelsea. The bus ride to NYU. I concentrated on slowing my breathing and getting my pulse down. I imagined lying on the bottom bunk and listening Chelsea's soft snore.

Go home, Casey. You can do this.

After ten minutes my bladder demanded that I find a bathroom. I let out a frustrated breath. Did I really think it would work the first time I tried it?

I knew better than to search for a room with indoor plumbing; I'd have to take this task outside. At the bottom of the stairs, I could hear the Ricci family eating dinner in the kitchen. I searched for the back door and stepped outside.

Before I could make it to the outhouse, I was hit was a wave of dizziness and a flash of light. Next thing I knew, I was back in my apartment, leaning against the front door.

Chelsea was curled up on our small sofa with a book in hand, waiting up for me. "You're back," she said. "I didn't even hear you come in."

"I didn't want to wake you." I was thankful for the dim lighting since I knew I would have the tell-tale dark circles under my eyes I always had after tripping.

Chelsea didn't seem to notice. Her pale brows jumped with anticipation and she said in a sing-song voice, "So, how was your date?"

I rubbed my forehead to ease the headache that was forming. "It was fine. He's a nice guy."

"Did he kiss you goodnight?"

"Yeah."

"Are you going to see him again?"

"Probably."

She cheered. "So exciting!"

I pumped a fist, like I was cheering, too. "But the movie was so loud, I have a headache now. I have to go lie down."

Disappointment crossed Chelsea's face. "Oh, well. You can tell me all about it in the morning."

Winters were just as cold in New York as they were in Boston. I studied hard and did well on my exams. Brendan and I had become a "thing," though we'd never really clarified the nature of our relationship. I couldn't bring myself to call him my boyfriend even though we spent most of our free time together and people asked me about him when they saw me alone.

I fell into a strange routine of sleeping in a nineteenth-century-style middle-class dress. Chelsea laughed in my face the first time she saw it, thinking it was an old nightgown.

"Good-night, Grandma," she said.

I did this because every Saturday morning, before I was fully awake, I attempted a controlled trip to the past. Knowing the Riccis were there for me gave me comfort. On the Saturday before winter break, it actually worked.

One moment I was in my bunk and the next, an empty lot.

I found the Riccis, and they welcomed me in. I stayed long enough to help the sisters serve fall harvest soup and homemade bread to soldiers on leave from the war, something they'd started doing as the weather grew colder. It took me a couple days, but I finally succeeded to bring on a controlled trip back to my present. It was the first time I'd managed to do it while standing up.

I went back to Cambridge for Christmas. Tim wanted to hear all about my tripping adventures and was encouraged to hear about how uneventful it was.

"It's so unusual for you to stay out of trouble," he said.

Lucinda wanted to hear all about Brendan.

"So how's it going? Is he good to you?" She sat on the edge of my bed and flicked her straight, dark hair over her shoulder. "You're pretty quiet on the subject."

"It's going good. He's nice enough." I plumped the pillows on my bed behind my back, trying to get comfortable. "We get along. It's okay."

Lucinda gaped. "Yikes."

"What?"

"*He's nice enough? We get along? It's okay?*" She swung her feet up onto the bed and tucked them under her thighs, yoga style. "Where's the passion, Casey? The spark? You definitely should be more excited."

"I know." I twisted a curl around my finger, not knowing how to explain. "It's just…"

"He's not Nate." Lucinda sighed and gave me sad puppy dog eyes. "You're not over him yet, are you?"

I shook my head. "I'm trying, but, no."

She patted my leg. "There's only one thing we can do to remedy this."

"Yeah, what's that?"

Lucinda sprung off the bed and grabbed her winter jacket. "Go shopping!"

There had been years when Lucinda and I practically lived at the mall. Mostly during our middle school years, when we were both geeky and awkward, me with long, pointy grasshopper-like limbs, and her with a mouthful of metal. When other kids were going to parties and movies and burger joints in groups, Lucinda and I had window-shopped, a lonely duo. Neither of us had money to do any real shopping outside of an order of fries or a sundae at the food court up on the second level of the mall.

We stopped at the store to thumb through the racks of clothes. She sighed wistful. "This always brings back so many memories."

I remembered bringing a stupefied Willie Watson to this shop, and how annoyed I felt at Lucinda for flirting with him. Now the memory made me smile.

We left the store and I paused at the rail to peer down at the Christmas shoppers flooding the floor below. The mall was decked out in festive reds and greens and bright, white lights. Holiday music bled through the chatter and shuffle of the crowd of shoppers.

"I'm hungry," Lucinda said.

"Me, too. But I'd rather not go to the food court." Not all my memories of the mall were happy ones. Too many memories of Nate. Some especially significant ones

237

at the food court.

Lucinda nodded, catching on. "Of course. Let's go somewhere else. There's a new bistro a little ways from here."

We were already on the escalator going down when I saw him. He'd stepped on the escalator going up, his face mirroring my startled look when he spotted me. We were trapped, pressed in by Christmas shoppers loaded down with shopping bags. There was no way we could avoid passing each other.

Lucinda whispered in my ear. "Oops."

I dry-swallowed. He just looked so... good. His hair was shorter, and his sideburns more defined, but his eyes were still that intense blue. They were locked on me.

Stay calm, Casey.

Things seemed to move both quickly and in slow motion at the same time, making my ears buzz.

I offered a slight smile and then looked away, my heart thudding. Despite my better judgment, I couldn't keep my gaze from flicking back to him. His eyes were still on me.

He nodded slightly in acknowledgment in the moment we passed each other, him going up, me on my way down. He was so close I could've reached out and touched him. The earth was shifting and no one noticed. All the shoppers in heavy jackets, chatting with their companions, or staring at phones—none of them noticed the cracking of my heart.

With a snap of the fingers, the moment was gone. I stared ahead vacantly. My knees felt weak. My vision grew blurry.

Lucinda elbowed me. "Hey, you okay? Don't forget to step off the escalator. You'll create a domino effect if you fall."

I stepped off successfully, but I couldn't stop myself from looking back to the balcony of the second floor. My eyes scanned the crowd for a sign of Nate, but he was gone.

Chapter Twenty—Eight

I survived the holidays and did my best to forget about Nate Mackenzie once I was back in New York City. The anniversary of my catastrophic tripping event with Adeline in Hollywood approached. Resetting the time line, meeting Marlene and Lolly, my time with the Revere family, all of it happened in the last year. It felt like a lifetime ago.

I had hopped a bus to meet up with Brendan at Starbucks. He sounded solemn on the phone and I wondered if he had done poorly on an exam. He was struggling with a few courses, and I felt badly for him. Getting good marks didn't seem to be a problem for me: I did my best to encourage him.

Brendan knew my usual order and normally had my drink waiting for me at the table. This time he hadn't even gone inside. He had a wool cap pulled over his nearly bald head, a scarf around his neck and both hands stuffed inside the pockets of his fleece jacket. The tip of his nose was rosy. Mine also burnt crimson with the cold. The wind blew my curls in my face and I wiped them away with my mitten.

"What's up?" I said when I reached him.

"I want to break up."

I shook my head, surprised at his bluntness.

"It's not working for me anymore, and I don't want to lead you on."

"Cool. The band aid approach," I said flatly.

"I'm just being honest."

"Okay. Thanks for telling me in person." I spun on my heels and headed back to the bus stop.

Two boyfriends, twice dumped.

Strangely, I didn't feel sad. Or mad. Nothing. I liked Brendan. He was a nice guy. Just, like Lucinda said, no spark.

Over the next weeks, I threw myself into my studies, taking little time for a social life. Brendan had been a big part of orchestrating that and I'd made the mistake of only making friends with Brendan's friends and not making any of my own. Without Brendan, I was basically left with one friend. Chelsea.

She, however, had made friends with other people besides me. She was kind enough to ask me to come along with her once in a while, which I did, but after a while I started to make excuses. It wasn't that her friends weren't nice. I just didn't feel like being social.

I was working on an assignment for English Lit one

Saturday afternoon when I was interrupted by a knock on the door.

I pushed my laptop to the empty spot beside me on the couch and stumbled to the door. "Forgot your keys again?"

I opened the door fully expecting to find Chelsea flushing red with embarrassment and making apologies.

Instead I found Nate.

Nate. In the hallway of my building. In New York City. He stared at me with his bright blue eyes, his lips tugging up in a crooked smile.

"What are you doing here?" I blurted.

"I came to see you."

"Oh."

"Can I come in?"

I ran a hand through my curls, just now remembering that I hadn't brushed my hair, hadn't put on makeup, hadn't even changed out of my pajama pants. At least I'd brushed my teeth.

I stepped back as Nate walked into our small suite. A surreal moment.

"Can I get you something to drink?" I didn't know why I asked him that. It seemed so formal and polite.

"Sure. Water would be great."

"I only have tap."

"That's fine." He slid out of his winter coat and draped it over the arm of one of the chairs. I gulped. He looked like he planned to stay.

I filled a glass and held it out to him, hoping he didn't notice the slight tremble in my hand. He sat in the chair by

242

his coat. I folded my legs beside me on the couch across from him.

"So, you came to see me?" I prompted.

"Lucinda told me you broke up with your boyfriend."

Wow. Thanks Luce. "Yeah, well, he actually broke up with me, but I was fine about it. We weren't really a good match."

His face pinched like he didn't like hearing me talk about another guy, even if it was about how things ended.

His eyes latched onto mine. "I'm glad to hear it."

His intensity made me squirm.

"How's BU?"

"Good. And NYU?"

I nodded. "Good."

"Good." Nate's eyes scanned the small space and I was suddenly self-conscious about the mess. Our apartment had a lived-in look.

"I don't go out much."

Oh, man. Why did I say that? It sounded pathetic.

The dead space was awkward. I wondered if I should put some music on or something. "How was the drive down?"

"Fine. Roads were clear for the most part." He leaned closer. "Are you hungry? It's been a while since I ate."

I was too nervous to be hungry. Besides, my brain was just catching up to having Nate in my living room.

"Can I take you out for dinner?" Nate's face was tight, like he was afraid I'd say no. I smiled to reassure him. "Okay. But I get to pick the place."

I took him to Ricci's Italian restaurant. Yes, *that* Ricci's. The old produce store space was now a compact but cozy restaurant with stucco and wood ceilings and walls, terracotta tile floors and red and white checkered table cloths. Small candles burned as center pieces.

A waiter took our order: thin crust cheese pizza with ham and tomatoes for me, and shrimp fettuccine for Nate.

"Quaint," Nate said, taking it in. "How'd you stumble on this place?"

"It's a long story."

He grinned. "I'm not in a hurry."

Because I knew Nate would want to know everything, I filled him in on all the details of my new alternate life with the Ricci's.

I remembered Leola's beau and his striking resemblance to Nate. "You don't happen to have German ancestry, do you?"

He wrinkled a brow. "I think my mother's grandparents or something might've been. Why?"

I grinned. "No reason."

"You can't imagine how relieved I am that you've found another family," he said.

I agreed. "They're good people."

Nate took a good look around. "So, this is their place?"

"Well, it looks a lot different in 1863," I said. "This section is a produce store. The kitchen area is in the same place, but it's simple without running water or stainless steel. The upper floors are occupied by the family, not rented out as office space."

"I'd like to go with you some day."

I felt my jaw drop open. I snapped it close.

"Casey, I want to try again. I know I was the one who said enough, but I was wrong. Maybe it's too late for us, but I hope not." He took a deep breath and squinted his eyes. He was nervous. I wasn't used to seeing him this way.

"Why didn't you call me at Christmas time? After you saw me at the mall."

"I knew you had a boyfriend."

I held in a smirk. He'd been checking up on me.

"I know I told you to get one." He rubbed the back of his neck and grimaced. "But I'll be honest with you. I hated it. Really, really hated it."

I bit the inside of my cheek to hold back the grin that threatened to cross my face.

Nate let out a long, pre-confessional sigh. "You don't know how badly I've wanted to come to New York to tell you this. I just wanted to give you time."

A bloom of pure happiness blossomed in my belly, but I pursed my lips, playing coy. "Time is something I have a lot of."

"You know what I mean." He dug into his pocket and pulled out an old pocket watch. My heart stopped.

"I thought I'd lost that," I said.

"You did. And I found it." He turned it over and pushed it to the middle of the table. The candlelight flickered, illuminating the inscription.

Casey & Nate
A love that transcends time.

He reached across the table for my hand. "I still love you. I've never stopped." He looked at me with an intensity that made my heart race. "Do you…"

"Yes. I love you, too."

He scooted his chair around the table and leaned in to kiss me. I shivered at his touch, at the gentleness of his lips. My mind could barely keep up. I was kissing Nate! Nate and I were together again!

I was glad we had slowed things down. That we had given ourselves the opportunity to mature, and to change our minds about each other if need be. To discover what we wanted in life, and who we wanted to be. Who we wanted to be with.

Because now we were certain about *us*, and our love was just so sweet.

Nate broke our kiss and a happy grin spread across his face.

He paid the bill and we walked outside, pausing under the street lamp.

"You're sure you want to see New York in the nineteenth century?" I asked.

"I'm sure," he said.

I squeezed his bare hand with my own. "Then hold on."

He gave me a questioning look.

"Samuel taught me a few things," I said. I closed my eyes and relaxed into Nate's embrace.

We fell into a tunnel of light.

The End

About the Author

Elle is the bestselling author of fun, other-worldy YA: whimsical things like time-travel, fairies and merfolk (with a nice helping of romance!) She divides her time between BC, Canada and Dresden, Germany, and enjoys drinking coffee and eating chocolate in both places. She also writes contemporary romance and speculative fiction as Lee Strauss.

Books by Elle Strauss

Clockwise
ClockwiseR
Like Clockwork
Clocked
Counter Clockwise
Clockwork Crazy

Seaweed

Love, Tink
(the complete series)

Elle Strauss

Acknowledgments

I can't tell you how much I love Casey & Nate and how much I've enjoyed writing their story. Finishing the series is bittersweet – I know it's time to move on, but I hate to say good-bye! So many good folk helped me on this journey and I've thanked them all along the way as each book was released, grateful from the bottom of my heart.

Many thanks for the support I get from my husband Norm, my kids, Joel, Levi, Jordan and Tasia, my parents, my IRL friends and my many online writing community friends—couldn't have done this without you!

A special thank-you to Angelika Offenwanger for seeing me through to the end as a beta reader, my editor and my friend.

And as always, thank you to God, for daily grace and mercy.

SEAWEED

CHAPTER ONE

HE STOOD at the bonfire with his head high, shoulders back, radiating a military type of confidence. With one hand he swept his dark hair across his forehead and even through the flickering orange hue I could tell he had amazing eyes.

Something drew his gaze to mine. Fate? Providence? My heart stopped beating. He smiled shyly then glanced away, his focus returning to the erratic dancing of the flames.

I'd never seen him before which, in Eastcove New Brunswick, was an unusual occurrence.

My best friends, Samara and Becca, stood beside me, each with a can of Coke in their hands.

"Who is that?" Samara shouted over the noise of the music blaring from a truck that was backed up close to the pit. Four teens sat squeezed together on the tailgate laughing at someone's joke.

Becca shouted back, "I think it's a *new* guy."

Samara fiddled with her long black braid. "Since when does anyone new move to Eastcove?"

Good question.

"He's cute!" Becca said.

"I saw him first." I gave him a little finger wave and started to make my way to the other side of the fire. I meant to clearly establish my intentions to claim this new boy.

I was intercepted by Colby Johnston.

"Hey, Seaweed." He moved in a little too close for comfort. I took a subtle step sideways.

"Hi."

I couldn't stop twisting my neck, watching the mysterious new guy. Another girl was chatting him up and a tickle of irritation curled up in my gut.

"What're you looking at?" Colby's gaze followed mine. "Ah, him."

I couldn't believe I hadn't heard about *him* already. Eastcove was a dying fishing village, the kind of town people *left*. A new family would've definitely made the gossip hotline.

"So, about us?" Colby said, like he'd said it a thousand times. Which he had.

I took a sip from my water bottle and tried to pretend I didn't hear him.

"Dori. We need to talk about this."

I let out a frustrated sigh. "Okay, talk."

He swigged back his drink, then spoke into my ear, "I know you already know this, but I guess I always thought we'd get together sometime. Sometime soon."

I did know this. I think everybody knew this. We were swim team champions. We were good friends. Even Samara and Becca thought we'd make the perfect couple.

Colby's dark eyes reflected the jumping flames, and I resisted the urge to reach over and rub his buzz cut, wanting to make everything okay.

Instead, I shook my head softly. "I'm sorry." I hated hurting him. I couldn't help that I didn't feel the same way.

His head fell forward. "I know, Seaweed. Forget I said anything." He slipped away, losing himself in the crowd. I blew out a heavy sigh.

The flames of the bonfire licked high toward the murky, open sky. The burning wood snapped and popped at its base. Smoke meshed with the salty essence of the sea and I breathed it in slowly. Peering through the sparks I kept my focus on the mystery guy. He caught me looking at him and this time he didn't look away. We gradually moved toward each other, until finally we were side by side.

"Hey."

"I'm Dori Seward," I said, loudly.

"Dori?"

"Yeah, like the fish in the movie." Did I really just say that? "It's a nickname because I like to swim. A lot." Okay, so much for smooth. Just kill me now.

He motioned for us to move away from the music toward the waves slapping the shore.

"It's a little quieter over here," he said. Then he shook my hand. "I'm Tor Riley." It was warm and strong.

"Where did you move from?" I asked, tucking my hands back into my pockets.

"Maine."

"So, you're not that far from home."

"I guess. I still have the Bay of Fundy."

He sipped his soda and I relieved my dry throat with my water.

"What do you think of Eastcove so far?"

He shrugged. "It's okay."

"What brought your parents here?" I knew there wasn't much left for work.

Tor fussed at the sand with his shoe. "Uh, I'm not here with them. They, uh, travel a lot. I'm living with my uncle."

I got the impression it was a touchy subject.

"What about you?" he said, turning the tables. "Tell me about you."

We headed back toward the warmth of the bonfire as I gave him the rundown of my average family—a mom, a dad, two brothers. I was about to broach the less than exciting topic of pets when I was interrupted by shouting and loud laughter on the other side of the fire pit. Sawyer shook his can and let the contents fly. Mike got him back with his drink, and before long everyone was in on it.

I looked at Tor and he smirked. That was when I did the stupidest thing ever. I opened my water bottle and swung it at Tor, splashing him right in the face.

I thought it would be funny. It was all in the name of fun and games. But instead of laughing and throwing his soda back at me, he looked at me with wide, horror-filled eyes.

Next thing I knew, Tor was sprinting down the beach into the darkness.

"Tor!" I yelled. With all the shouting, the blaring music, and the roar of waves crashing to shore, no one heard me.

"Tor!" I took off after him, and in the mayhem, no one noticed. "I'm sorry. Please, come back."

I could make out his outline in the moonlit darkness when I followed him around the bend. My heart raced and I wanted to tackle him to the ground until he told me what was going on.

I didn't have a chance. I got to a cropping of rocks just in time to see him dive into the frigid ocean.

Find out more about Elle Strauss and follow her on social media by visiting www.**ellestraussbooks.com**

Made in the USA
Charleston, SC
08 June 2016